THIS LITTLE PIG

by Janette Oke

Illustrated by Brenda Mann

Edited by Grace Pettifor

Other Janette Oke
Children's Books in this Series:

Spunky's Diary
New Kid In Town
The Prodigal Cat
Ducktails
The Impatient Turtle
A Cote of Many Colors
A Prairie Dog Town
Maury Had a Little Lamb
Trouble in Fur Coat
Pordy's Prickly Problem
Who's New at the Zoo?

Published by Bethany House Publishers
A Ministry of Bethany Fellowhship International
11400 Hampshire Avenue South
Minneapolis, Minnesota 55438
www.bethanyhouse.com

Cover Illustration by
Brenda Mann

Printed in the United States of America

ISBN 0-934998-43-4

Dedicated with love
to Alexander Nicolas Logan
who joined our family on December 27, 1990,
a new son for Marvin and Laurel
and a baby brother for Nate, Jessica and Jacquelyn.
And to Kristalyn Lorene Oke
born on February 7, 1991,
daughter of Lorne and Debbie
and baby sister for Katie.

May God bless our time together.

TABLE OF CONTENTS

CHAPTER ONE
A NEW WORLD

It was noisy! The air around me was filled with high-pitched squeals, rustling of straw, and soft, low, grunting sounds. For a moment I shook my head in confusion and then I tried to block out all other sounds and concentrate on the coaxing grunts. Somehow I knew instinctively that they were meant for me.

I don't know which feeling was the most intense. The one in my stomach - that told me with sharp, insistent rumblings that I was hungry - or the need to follow the grunting sounds that drew me to seek out the one from whence they came. How was I to know that the two were linked together?

I shuffled up on shaky feet and wiggled my way through the straw. It wasn't deep, but it did impede my progress and twice it even had me scrambling to get back on my feet again.

Squeals bombarded my sensitive ears again. Much to my surprise I discovered that the noise was coming from my own mouth. I hushed it for a minute - and then decided that I needed it. Needed it to communicate with the one making the low soft grunts.

At last I managed to reach the source of the sounds and we exchanged greetings.

"Are you okay?" she asked me.

"I - I think so," I squealed back in my high squeaky voice. I wondered if it sounded as funny to her as it did to me. I had never used my voice before and wasn't used to the sound it made.

"Good," she said and she kissed me on the nose. "Good."

Soft brown eyes checked me carefully as she gently nudged me. I could feel the warmth of her breath and the coolness of her kisses as she brushed me with her snout. At last she seemed satisfied that I was really okay and she spoke again. "You're fine. Just fine." The brown eyes twinkled as she said it. She was beautiful! "Now you'd better get some dinner," she said.

"Dinner? Where?"

"Just join the others. You'll find it," and she laid her head back down on the soft straw.

I went to where all the noise and commotion was coming from. Sure enough, after pushing my way around a bit, I found some dinner.

I was so busy eating that I hardly noticed those around me. Later I discovered they were my brothers and sisters. I would be eating dinner with them for some time to come. But that did not concern me in the least as I enjoyed my very first meal. That is, until I found myself being pushed around. A new member had joined us. He was bigger than myself and he seemed terribly hungry and not very polite.

"Move over," he squealed. "It's my turn. Mother said for me to find dinner."

I wasn't smart enough to know that if I opened my mouth to reply, I would lose possession of my meal ticket.

"She told me that, too," I informed him. "But this is mine. You find your own."

I turned back to grab my dinner again only to find that he had already taken over. Boy, was I mad! I squealed and cried and tried to kick him away with my front and hind feet but he was too busy to care and too big to push. Soon I realized that if I was going to fill my hungry tummy I had to locate a new spot where no big bully was taking over the menu.

It took me a while to find another place to nurse and, when I finally did, I was so hungry and so angry that my stomach was roiling for more than one reason. I settled in and began to make up for the time I had lost. My tummy began to feel more comfortable and I found it easy to block out the sounds and movements around me. I was so tired and comfortable that I just snuggled up against the safe, warm side of my mother. I guess I had a little nap.

Something strange touching my sides awakened me. Before I knew what was happening I felt myself being lifted up - up - up. I didn't think that I was ever going to stop. When I opened my eyes my heart gave a flip. There I was dangling way up above the soft straw-covered floor. I let out a terrified squeal in protest but the hands that held me drew me up against something soft, yet solid, and held me snugly. I felt a little better and safer then.

"What's the matter little fella?" a voice asked. I thought it a foolish question. Who wouldn't have objected to being suspended in mid-air in such a fashion?

The hands holding me moved to scratch behind my ear and gently rub my back. I liked the feeling though I wasn't sure why.

"You're a pretty nice little fella," the voice went on and I could sense approval in the tone. "I think the kids would like to see you."

I didn't know who the "kids" were and he didn't answer me when I asked. He just started moving toward an open door and I felt myself being snuggled into new warmth.

"I'll just tuck you here in my jacket," the voice continued. "The wind might be a bit cool for your new little hide."

I closed my eyes again. The gentle movement made my tummy a bit squeamish. But soon I got used to it and I was ready to sleep again.

I would have slept but, just as I was about to doze off, we reached wherever we were going. The movement stopped and I heard the voice again.

"Guess what I've got."

Another, shriller voice responded.

"What? What you got? C'mon, Daddy. Don't tease. Show us."

And then a whole chorus of voices began to scream almost in my ear.

"Show us! Show us, Daddy! C'mon, show us what you got."

I squirmed a bit, struggling to crawl a little deeper into the safety of the jacket. Before I had moved far, the hand was lifting me out into the bright light and the noise.

"A pig! A baby pig!" the voices screamed in excitement.

"When was he born?" someone asked in a little softer tone.

"Just a short while ago. He's just had his first dinner."

"Oh, let me hold him."

As soon as the words were out there were more screams and bodies began to press against us. Voices added to the din, "Let me hold him. Let me hold him. Can I hold him? Please?"

"Just a minute," responded the big voice. "He is very new. You'll have to be careful. You'll need to take turns."

I was deposited in a lap and two very small hands held me rather awkwardly. It wasn't as comfortable as the inner jacket had been but the hands seemed delighted and they really caused me no harm.

"How many in the litter?" the soft voice asked.

"Seven."

"Seven? Not the best that she's done - but not bad. Are they all healthy looking?"

"There is one runt but another fella who makes up for it. He's a big one. Then this one - and four little females."

I was passed to another pair of hands. They stroked me softly and rubbed gently on my ear. "He's cute," said another voice.

The hand shifted to tug gently on my curly tail.
I was about to protest but the big voice did it for me.

"Don't pull his tail. Just pat him like this."

The hands began to rub along my back again.

"Now it's Jill's turn."

There was a squeal of protest but the big voice
was firm.

"Jason, you have had your turn. It must go back
to its mama soon. You let Jill have her turn now."

The little voice still was not in agreement. Nor
were the hands. As the big hands reached to lift me
away, the little hands clutched firmly to me. I was
afraid that I would be pulled asunder but the big
voice said, "Jason!" The little voice began to wail
but the little hands let go.

I was passed to new hands. They were not nearly
as big as the biggest hands, but there was a gentle-
ness, a protectiveness there that I sensed immediately. I liked the feel of them.

"You are cute," she crooned to me and I knew
that it was the voice that I had heard say the same
words earlier.

The hands slid over my sides, over my back, up
my neck and behind my ears. Each touch was gentle,
yet probing.

"He's nice, Dad," the voice said. "Do you think
he's the one for my project?"

"I wondered about that when I saw him. If he
develops like he should, he could well be. He has
good proportions. There's also the larger one to
consider. We'll have to watch them grow."

"He's cute," the voice insisted.

"Well, we'll keep an eye on them and see what happens," said the big voice. "Now I'd better get him back out to the barn to his ma. He'll soon be wanting to eat again."

The very words made my stomach rumble. I was hungry again. I hadn't realized it until he had made the remark. Now I couldn't wait to get back to my mother.

The ride back was not nearly as scary and the distance didn't seem as far. I didn't even try to snuggle down inside the jacket for a sleep. I could think of only one thing. He was taking me back to my "ma" and he said that I would be able to eat again. I was ready for that. I was already starved.

CHAPTER TWO
FAMILY

The first thing I did upon reaching my mother was to settle in and eat my fill again. I didn't pay any attention to the squirming, complaining squealers who were already there. I just went to work and drank until I was full and then snuggled up with the rest of them and had a good, long sleep.

It was the big guy who woke me up. He was hungry again and didn't seem to care one bit who he climbed over in order to find some dinner.

"Hey, watch it," I squealed angrily at him. "You almost stepped in my eye."

"Well get your eye outta the way," he answered in a real sassy voice.

"My eye is where it's supposed to be," I informed him. "It's your foot that's out of place."

"Quit your..."

But Mother's voice cut in. "There is plenty for everyone," she informed us both. "Don't quarrel. Please. You disturb everyone when you fuss."

The words were firm but the love in her voice took all of the sting out of them. It was true. I could hear my siblings stirring. It wasn't long until we were all awake. The squealing and jostling for

position started all over again and continued until everyone had found a spot for dinner. Then things got quiet again and I think I even heard my mother snoring softly. I had a good nap and didn't awaken until I was hungry again.

I was soon to make the acquaintance of the rest of the family members. Mother was the big, strong, cushiony one, of course, and the rest were brothers and sisters. In our "litter" we had three boys and four girls.

Mother introduced us to one another as soon as we could keep our eyes open long enough to pay close attention to her.

"I want you to meet your sisters and brothers," she said to all of us. "I will start in order of your birth. This is the first born, Othelia."

Mother pointed her snout at a girl who stood slightly apart from the rest of us. The sister squirmed at the attention, seeming real pleased with herself. I recognized her as the one who could do a good job of pushing when it came to the dinner table. But we all said "hello" and then Mother went on.

"And this is Tillie - and beside her, Millie."

As I looked at them I wondered if I'd ever learn to tell them apart. They looked exactly alike to me. I had wondered previously if there were really two of them - or if I was seeing double. But there they both were, snuggling close together and grinning silly little nervous grins. We said our "hellos" again.

"Then we have Hiram."

It took a minute before I realized that Mother was pointing her nose at me. All eyes turned toward me and I began to squirm uncomfortably. Almost immediately Mother turned and went on with the introductions.

"And then Hawkins," Mother said with a shake of her head toward the big one.

"The bully," I said under my breath, but aloud I said "hello," though my eyes held a bit of a challenge. It gave me satisfaction to know the name of the one I'd been fighting for position. Now I could yell out his name and give him a heave with my shoulder. Maybe he felt the same way. As we all said our "hellos" his eyes held mine and he didn't flinch or blink.

"Next," said Mother, "we have Bee-Bee."

It was strange name but the bearer wore it proudly. Her head came up and she gave us the most confident smile. There was no nervous squirming, no lowering of the eyes, no girlish giggle of embarrassment. She met our eyes candidly. There was such a light in hers that I knew instinctively that she was going to be a lot of fun.

"And finally," said Mother, "Higgins."

Higgins was much smaller than the rest of us. Standing beside Hawkins like he was now, he looked even smaller. But he had spunk and, as we said our "hellos," I saw his shoulder go up against the leg of our big brother. I knew that he was bracing himself for a dash just as soon as Mother had finished speaking. I guess he figured that it was time to eat again.

I took one more look around the circle. "Othelia. Tillie and Millie - or is it Millie and Tillie? I'm not sure. Then me - Hiram, Hawkins, Bee-Bee and Higgins," I said softly under my breath. It seemed important to remember each of my family by name - now that I knew they each had a name. I reviewed them all one more time. Then, keeping an eye on Higgins, I also prepared to dash forward the moment that Mother laid down on our straw bed.

The days passed quickly. I became very attached to Mother even when I wasn't having dinner. She talked to us at times. She would lower her head close to ours and I could see her soft, brown eyes as she spoke. At first it was very gentle, coaxing and caressing us with her voice. Soon the words were more direct: hushing us when we got too demanding, scolding us when we argued about who was being pushy, and instructing us about our new surroundings.

We slept, awoke, scrambled for our next meal, ate hungrily and slept again. Now and then Mother rolled up onto her feet, shook us all free and turned to the feeding trough that was there for her. We heard her eat and drink noisily. Then she would grunt a few times, nose us all aside and flop down in the straw again. As soon as she was settled, we would all squeal our way to her side and snuggle up against her again.

As we grew we became more and more curious about our surroundings. Mother listened to our questions and answered whatever we asked.

"Where is this place?" one of the girls asked her

when we were a few days old. I don't know if it was Millie or Tillie. I just call both of them "Sister."

"This is the barn - or, rather, the shed attached to the barn."

"Are we the only ones who live here?"

I could have answered that. I had already seen some strange creatures stirring about in our shed.

"Oh, no," said Mother. "Many animals live here."

"What kind of animals?" asked the inquisitive one.

"More pigs. Cows. Horses. A dog. Cats. Then there are the fowl."

"Fowl?"

"Chickens. Geese. Turkeys."

"Where are they?" asked the sister, her eyes darting here and there with a frightened look. The thought of so many animals must have scared her.

"In the barn. In the barnyard. Over in the hen house and chicken coop," answered Mother, not one bit concerned.

"I saw one in here," I butted in. "I really did. Saw it myself."

"Where?" asked my scaredy-cat sister.

"Right up there," I said, pointing at the high fence around our pen with the tip of my snout. "It was sitting right up on that rail. Then it jumped down on the other side and went away."

"That would have been Cat," said Mother. Then she turned around casually and dipped her nose in her trough, taking a long, deep drink of whatever was there.

"Does Cat hurt us?" asked my sister.

Mother didn't answer until she was finished drinking. She smacked once or twice and turned to smile at the little one. "Oh, my, no," she said. "Cat pays little attention to us at all."

Sister looked relieved.

"Why does she come here?" asked Sister. I wasn't sure if it was Millie or Tillie.

"She was likely looking for Mouse."

"Mouse?" The second one of the pair had moved in close and taken over the questions.

Mother shoved her nose back in the trough and came up noisily smacking again.

"What are Mouse?" asked one of the shaking pair.

"Mice?" said Mother around a bit of something she seemed to be enjoying.

"I thought you said Mouse," said one of the girls.

"Mouse, yes. That's one. When there are more than one, they are called Mice," explained Mother.

"Are they...are they in here?" shivered the sister, pressing tightly against her look-alike.

"Sometimes," answered Mother. She did not seem the least concerned. I wondered why I had never seen them. I had seen Cat.

"Why...why don't we see them?" quivered one of the pair.

"They are quite small. Quite small," answered Mother.

"Why does Cat want to see them?" asked a new voice and I turned to see that Bee-Bee had joined us.

"Why, Cat makes dinner of them," Mother replied matter-of-factly.

"Dinner?" three voices said in unison.

Mother nodded her head and the long, green, leafy thing that she was eating waved under her chin.

"Are they good?" asked Bee-Bee.

"Cat thinks so," Mother replied and went back to chomping on her own dinner.

There was silence for a minute and then Bee-Bee spoke up. "Could we try them?" she asked.

Mother stopped her chewing and looked at Bee-Bee in surprise. Then she shook her head slowly and began to chew again. "I don't think so," she said. "I don't think that you'd like them at all."

"Have you tried them?" asked Bee-Bee.

Mother shook her head again. "No," she admitted. "I have never tried them."

"Then how do you know?" asked Bee-Bee candidly.

Mother didn't seem to have a good answer. At last she spoke almost absent-mindedly, "Cat eats Mice. We eat other things."

"What other things?" asked Hawkins, pushing his way into the space and the conversation.

"Well," said Mother without missing a bite in her chewing, "almost every other thing."

I don't know if that satisfied Bee-Bee but she didn't ask any more questions.

It wasn't quite good enough for me. I had only tried eating one thing - though Mother certainly seemed to enjoy all of the strange smells and shapes that she pulled from her trough. Something within me made me very impatient to try some of those delicacies, too.

"And who knows," I whispered to myself, "I might even decide to try Mouse. If Cat likes it, then I might like it."

My thoughts were interrupted by the opening of the barn door. The same animal that had visited us over the days since our arrival came in. It was the one with the kind hands and gentle voice. Mother called it "Girl."

Mother did not seem the least bit nervous when Girl made her appearance. We soon learned that we didn't need to high-tail it into the furthest corner and try to bury ourselves in the straw like we had done at first.

"Good morning, Mrs. White Sow," Girl said to Mother and leaned over the pen to scratch behind Mother's ear. Mother grunted her pleasure.

"How are your piglets?" Girl asked next, still busily scratching behind Mother's ear. "I see they are growing quickly. You must be taking good care of them," she went on, not waiting for Mother's answer.

Then she climbed over the boards that separated us from the rest of the shed and headed straight for the corner where we huddled together. As usual, it was me that she scooped up.

"And how are you, Piggy?" she asked me. "I think you are going to make a fine porker. I can hardly wait for you to be big enough to play with."

I was a bit put out with her calling me "Piggy." My name was Hiram. My mother had told me so

herself. Who should know better than Mother? And this "Porker" bit. Mother had already informed us that we were pigs. Porker, indeed!

"Daddy says your brother is going to be bigger and maybe I should choose him for my project, but I like you. You're cuter."

I didn't know what she meant, but I liked the idea of her choosing me. The soft hands rubbed my sides and stroked my back. Then they moved to scratch behind my ear and I knew why Mother grunted with satisfaction whenever Girl scratched her in such a way. It felt just wonderful. I wanted to curl up against Girl's strange-smelling softness and fall fast asleep while enjoying the luxury of being caressed.

Before my eyelids had a chance to close, I was gently lowered to the straw bed again and Girl was moving away.

"I'll see you tomorrow," she called over her shoulder. "I have to do my chores now."

The door closed behind her and I stood blinking in disappointment. Perhaps Mother felt the same way. She turned away from her trough and headed for the straw bed. Flopping down on the softness, she wiggled her nose back and forth in the straw.

"Come!" she called to us. "It's nap time."

We didn't need to be invited twice. We all ran for Mother. Hawkins butted up against me even harder than usual nearly knocking me off my feet. I righted myself and gave him a dirty look. Then I noticed the look in his eyes. I knew that he had heard everything Girl had said. I thrust out my chin and moved forward defiantly but he pushed me again and ran to Mother. I raced after him. He had already claimed his spot and I shoved him with my snout just to let him know that I didn't appreciate being pushed around.

"Hey!" he hollered, but he didn't let go of his hold.

I quickly by-passed him and hurried to find my own spot before they were all taken.

Then I reminded myself that there was room for all of us. Never had Mother been short at dinnertime yet, but we always fought over our meals as though someone was sure to be left out.

CHAPTER THREE
GROWING

I knew that I was growing. I could sense the new sturdiness of my body and see my filled-out sides. My legs were stronger and my meals less frequent with more time between eating and naps. As the days passed, I became more and more curious about the shed in which we lived. I spent time sniffing my way around our little enclosure trying to discover new smells and sights. Hawkins shared my curiosity. If I discovered something interesting, he quickly nosed me aside and took over the investigation.

I resented his rude bullying but there wasn't much I could do about it except to squeal and grouch whenever he started to throw his weight around. It didn't do much good because he was still bigger than I was. Once, when he had forced his way roughly by me, I called angrily after him, "You might be bigger...but...but Girl says I'm cuter."

He was facing me in a moment, glaring into my eyes angrily, "Don't you ever say that to me again, do you hear? Or...or we'll see who's cuter. I'll... I'll make you sorry for thinking you're so...so great."

I decided not to mention the fact again but he couldn't stop me from thinking about it. Whenever Girl came to visit, both of us tried to make her notice us. Whatever her project was, we didn't want the other one chosen for it.

I concentrated on eating. I had heard Mother remark to Higgins that he should be sure to eat well so he would grow big and strong. I figured what applied to Higgins should also apply to me. In my dreams I saw myself catching up to Hawkins and then by-passing him until I was much bigger than he was. I imagined myself towering over him, bullying him into moving aside for me, or just tramping right over the top of him.

I always relished those dreams but was disappointed when I opened my eyes and discovered that I was still the "little" brother. No matter how much I ate, Hawkins was always able to eat more.

One day the big voice came to the shed. We had learned from Mother that his name was Man. We were not afraid of him. Mother seemed quite anxious to see him whenever the door opened. I felt that it had something to do with the pail he usually carried full of strange-smelling things that Mother considered delicious. Often he stopped to rub her back or scratch behind her ears. Mother seemed to enjoy that too.

This time he had no pail in his hand.

"How would you like to take your little ones out to see some sunshine?" he asked Mother as he scratched behind her left ear.

She grunted that she would be delighted but he

went right on as though she had not spoken.

"I know they are young - but it's a beautiful day and I think it would be good for them. What do you say?"

Mother assured him that we were quite old enough and healthy enough to go out.

"I won't tell you to keep their feet dry - that would be impossible. There isn't a dry place to put your foot out there. But, if the sun keeps shining like it is today, it'll be dry soon enough."

I knew that Mother was eager to get out and his incessant talking was hard on her patience.

"Well, you gather those young ones up and I'll open your door," said Man. He lifted one of his long, long legs over the pen boards and settled it inside our domain. I couldn't believe how he climbed our fence. Girl always scampered from one board to the next until she reached the top and then she scampered down the other side. Not him. He just lifted that long leg, swished it over the top board and planted it right down on the other side. Then the next leg followed and there he was, inside our pen.

We all ran squealing into a corner and huddled together, even though we knew that he wouldn't harm us. I guess we were all surprised at the suddenness with which he came.

In a few quick strides he was at the far side of our enclosure. He leaned over and worked with something, then pushed with his foot. Mother was right at his heels and I wondered if she would push him out of the way in her impatience.

She didn't, but I felt within me that she found it hard to resist.

Then the strangest thing happened. With the push of his foot a small squeaky door swung slowly outward and a bright light streamed in. We piglets ducked our heads and shut our eyes against it, but Mother didn't. I heard her call for us to gather ourselves together and follow. There was rustling of the straw and footsteps. I knew that she was moving out of the pen as quickly as she could.

I opened my eyes. I didn't want to be left behind. I had no idea where the door would take Mother but I didn't want to be left without her. With a squeal I hurled myself at the door and my sisters and brothers came squealing after me. I was afraid that we might already have lost sight of Mother but, to my relief, she was just a few paces beyond the door. Her nose was in the air as she sniffed and smacked, seeming to smell and taste the air at the same time.

I slid to a stop between her back feet. The bright light was still hurting my eyes and the shadow from her large frame made it easier to adjust to the dazzle. From my safe place under her, I squinted and tried to bring things into focus. It was a whole new, strange world that we had entered. I could hear Millie and Tillie whimpering softly as they pressed against Mother's front feet. Othelia looked boldly out at the new world with a cockiness that I had never seen before. Bee-Bee smiled softly as though she couldn't wait to see what all was in store. Higgins pressed himself closer to Mother's leg, peering out with blinking eyes.

Only Hawkins stood alone. His legs were spread apart and his eyes were unblinking. He strutted forward a couple paces and planted his feet again. I knew that he felt quite able to take on whatever the new world could bring him.

Mother spoke and, though she included us all in her little speech, I knew that she was directing much of what she said to Hawkins.

"Now stay close to me. If I should call, come immediately without hesitation or argument. Don't go sticking your noses into dangerous places and don't interfere with any of our neighbors. Do you all understand?"

Her eyes were riveted on Hawkins as she asked the question with a firmness that I had never heard in her voice before.

His eyes fell slightly and I saw him squirm. I didn't wonder why. The face that usually held a calm, easy expression was now tight with seriousness. Mother seemed to want us all to understand the importance of staying close to her. Most of us had no intention of straying, but Hawkins was another matter. And it was Hawkins who was suffering the full intensity of her gaze because of it.

I wanted to giggle. It gave me pleasure to see him brought down to proper size. I was afraid if he saw me laughing he would get even with me later, so I put one of Mother's legs between my brother and myself so that I could hide my smirk.

Mother surprised me by moving that leg and I was bumped aside and left without cover. With a squeal I whirled around and followed her forward.

All of us were pressing against this foot or that so that she had to move forward with caution. She stopped again and I thumped my nose against her leg before I could slide to a stop.

I peered around her and there - not a pen length from her - were three of the largest animals I had ever seen in my life. My breath caught in my throat and I shut my eyes quickly. I was sure they would trample us or devour us before we could even make a move. But Mother was speaking.

"Good morning," she said politely.

"Good morning," they replied almost with one breath.

Then one of them spoke alone. "I see you have another family."

"Yes," said Mother with pride in her voice. "This is their first outing. Children, say hello."

We obeyed and the three big creatures greeted us as a unit rather than one by one.

Around the three big monsters, four small versions of the same type of animal galloped and bounded, careening wildly from side to side, then sliding to quick stops that lasted only a minute before they dashed off again.

One of the big animals spoke. "I have twins," she said proudly, and cast her eyes to the four running things. "The red and white ones - like their father."

There were two red and white ones in the frolicking foursome. The other two were black and white like the three big creatures before us.

Mother smiled. "How nice," she said politely.

"They are beautiful children. I'm so happy for you."

The animal seemed smug about her accomplishment. I looked at our family, all gathered around Mother's legs. I counted quickly. Seven. Why should this creature be so self-satisfied at having two, I wondered?

Then Mother turned to the other two creatures. "My, you have lovely young, too," she complimented them. "Such energy!"

They both seemed pleased with Mother's comment, but went right on munching on the long stringy stuff that dangled from their mouths until they could chew their way down the stems as they drew it all in.

Mother moved on and I scurried on as quickly as I could so that I could catch up to the front of her.

"Who was that?" I managed to ask even though I was out of breath.

"The Cow family," answered Mother.

"They are...big," I panted.

"Yes," said Mother, "but gentle."

I was glad to hear that.

"Do they live here, too?" I asked next.

"Oh, yes. They share the other end of the barn."

I cast a backward glance at the monster family as I ran, and bumped right into Mother's leg.

"Oops," said Mother. "Watch where you're going."

"Where *are* we going?" I puffed.

"To say hello to the other pigs," answered Mother. "It has been some time since I chatted with them."

"There are others?"

"Oh, yes. Didn't I tell you?"

Perhaps she had. I had to admit that I didn't always listen carefully when Mother was talking.

Before we got to wherever it was we were going to say hello to the other pigs, we met some more animals. These were even bigger than the Cow family. I couldn't believe my eyes.

There were two of them and they were walking single file down a path directly toward us. Of course Mother moved off to the side without argument, but she didn't turn tail and run. Nor did she seem particularly nervous. She just kept plodding along slowly in the same direction that she had been taking. On they came, great heads held high and shaking now and then. One of them lifted his head even higher and puffed out his nostrils, snorting loudly and shaking his head vigorously as he did so. I ducked quickly under Mother, scared half to death.

But Mother never even shivered. "Hello," she said civilly and they nodded their greetings in return.

They came abreast of us and then passed on down the path, their great feet causing the ground to tremble beneath us.

I wanted to run. I wanted to hide. But I wasn't going anywhere without Mother. I pressed up against her moving leg wherever I could push against it. It was difficult. There would be a moment's comfort as her foot touched the ground and then it would lift again and I would be bumped aside

and exposed to the frightening world. Then the foot would come down again and I would quickly press against it for instant comfort, then be brushed aside as it lifted again for the next step.

Bump and press, bump and press, we went on down the yard. I squealed in my frustration but Mother seemed to ignore me completely.

Once we were safely past the big animals, Mother moved over and took the path again. It was rutted and bumpy and the wetness splashed over my feet, up my legs and even on the underside of my tummy. Mother seemed to do quite well on it. She walked quickly and it was hard for us little ones to jump and bump our way over the uneven, slippery track.

"Who were they?" I heard Othelia ask Mother as soon as we were safely past the biggest monsters and I listened carefully. I had been wondering the same thing.

"The Horse family," answered Mother and there was no concern in her voice.

"Boy, they were big!" said Bee-Bee, her eyes wide with awe.

"Yes," said Mother. "They are the biggest animals on the farm."

I breathed a sigh of relief. At least we wouldn't be meeting anything bigger on the trail.

"Will they hurt us?" panted Higgins, and I could hear the fear in his shaky voice.

"Not as long as we stay out from under their big feet," said Mother.

I, for one, had no intention of getting anywhere near those big feet. I could still hear the ground tremble as they thudded past.

"Are we almost there?" panted Tillie - or Millie - and I knew that she was just about worn out from the long walk.

"Almost," said Mother, glancing down at us, concern in her voice. She slowed her steps slightly to accommodate our short legs and seemed to apologize that her excitement had pressed us forward at such a pace. "As soon as we say our 'hellos' you may have a rest and some dinner," she promised. I started off again on eager legs. It sounded good to me.

CHAPTER FOUR

OUR KIND

Mother's steps began to hasten again in spite of her attempt to slow down to our speed. I knew that she was excited about seeing her friends.

"We are almost there," I heard her say to little Higgins as she urged him on. His short legs had been particularly pressed in their effort to keep up with her.

Then I heard an excited call from somewhere ahead of us and Mother answered with equal enthusiasm.

"You're out," the voice called again and Mother called back, "Finally."

Two animals of Mother's size moved forward and all three thrust their noses forward, greeting one another with welcoming grunts, quick questions and rapid replies. Everyone was talking at once but no one seemed to mind.

At last the talk got around to us.

"Your family is growing quickly," said one.

"And yours," said Mother, pointing her snout at the young who busied themselves around a nearby trough.

"Yes," said Mrs. Red Sow. "They have grown

so quickly. I just can't believe it. It won't be long until they're on their own."

She seemed sad about that fact. I watched the fighting, clamoring family of eight and wondered why anyone would miss them. Why, they were almost half as big as their mother and not nearly as polite. Mother interrupted my thoughts. "Children, say hello," she instructed and we obediently chorused our greetings.

"How nice," smiled the third member of the group. She did not have a family, either pressing about her heels or rummaging at a near-by trough.

Mother turned to her. "And when is your family due, dear?" she asked.

The younger mother-to-be blushed prettily. "Soon," she said, "very soon. I'm hoping to be put in one of the barn pens any day now."

"How nice," said Mother as she smiled warmly at the other.

The conversation continued but I turned my interest to the trough and the half-grown family. Would the day come when we, too, would be able to eat from a trough? I had never thought about it before. I had just assumed that Mother would always feed us. But Mother seemed to enjoy the trough feeding so much. I couldn't help but think how wonderful it would be to sample it myself. And I was hungry. So hungry!

Then my attention was jerked back to the conversation when I heard Mother say, "Now if you'll just excuse me for a few minutes, I promised the children they could rest and eat as soon as we arrived."

"Of course," murmured the big red sow. "They need to eat to grow." She made the last statement with a chuckle and cast a glance toward her fighting brood again, pride in her voice. I knew she felt that hers had grown abnormally fast.

Mother moved off a few feet, found an acceptable spot where some straw had been piled to make a dry bed and flopped down on her side. As soon as she lowered herself to the ground we were there to find our positions. Mother squirmed her way right into the warmness and sighed as she closed her eyes against the bright sunlight. The comforting rays beat down upon our backs as we settled in to eat. I liked the feel of it. We had been warm in the barn shed, but something about the sun on our backs made this warmth feel different.

As soon as I had eaten my fill I snuggled up close against Mother. I couldn't remember ever feeling so comfortable in all of my life. The air smelled deliciously fresh. The sun bathed my body with caressing warmth. The rest of the family was contented and quiet rather than a squirming pack of kicking feet and pushing noses. In the distance I could hear the Cow family talking and the thumping feet of their galloping off-spring. Occasionally I heard a snort. I knew that not too far away the Horse family flung their heads and blew, but the big thundering feet no longer concerned me.

I was getting drowsy. It felt so good just to lie in the sun, tummy full, back warm and Mother with me. I closed my eyes and drifted off to sleep.

It seemed that I didn't sleep for long. The world was moving beneath me, shaking, shuddering, shifting. I opened my eyes quickly, about to squeal in fright, when I discovered that Mother had decided that it was time to get up.

In an instant we became a scrambling, squealing mass of scurrying feet and complaining voices. We scattered on the ground as Mother stood; some on our backs, some on our sides and some lucky enough to land on our feet.

Mother stood and shook herself, then started forward with lumbering steps.

The sun was hot overhead now, but the path that Mother took was still wet and muddy.

"Where are we going now?" cried Higgins.

"The sun is getting too hot," replied Mother. "We need to get out of it."

Even though I had thoroughly enjoyed the sun, shade sounded good to me. I feared that my one exposed side might have had a bit too much sun. It felt hot and uncomfortable.

Ahead of us I could see a low spot where dark mud stained the surface of the field. It looked wet and deep - like one could almost get buried in it. I hoped that Mother would see it in time to skirt it widely.

But Mother seemed to ignore the danger and was headed directly for the spot.

My eyes grew wider and wider. I was too scared to speak but I could not pull my gaze away from the miry place.

"Mother," I finally managed. "the...the mud."

Just as I choked out the word, something moved. The mud moved. I stopped dead in my tracks and held my breath. Mother kept right on walking with all of the litter but me at her heels.

"The mud," I squealed after them. "It's...it's alive."

The mud heaved again and up came a head. I wouldn't even have recognized it as a head, had not the eyes blinked. I had never seen live mud before.

Then the mouth opened and spoke - right to Mother.

"I wondered how long you would be. It's getting quite warm."

It was the voice of Mrs. Red Sow.

"Yes," Mother replied. "It is. But they needed their rest."

Without even slowing down Mother walked right on into that deep gooey mud and shoved her nose into it as though searching out a special place. We all clustered around the edge, frantic that it would swallow her up. Then, plop, down she went right on her side. The mud flew out in all directions as she lit. I blinked. We had all been splattered. I wanted to turn and run but I heard Bee-Bee giggle. I forced myself to open my eyes and take another look.

Mother was still there. She hadn't sunk out of sight after all. Her mouth was working as she smacked with satisfaction. Her eyes were closed against the heat and light and she had a contented look on her face.

"Ah-h. I have missed this," she sighed.

Another part of the mud moved and the young sow raised her head. "I'll miss it too," she stated but she didn't sound too worried about it. Perhaps she felt that her new family would more than make up for the loss of the mud hole.

Mother drew herself up far enough to roll over onto her other side. She squirmed her way deeper into the goo and shut her eyes again. "Why don't you come in?" she said softly and we knew she was speaking to us.

We looked from one to another. We were wondering which one of us would be brave enough to try it first.

It was Othelia who stepped forward. Her eyes showed her fear - but her determination as well. She took one step, then another. She was already up to her knees in mud. I saw her make a face. I don't think she liked it. She took another tentative step and grimaced again. We all waited. Suddenly there was a rush and a splash as Hawkins threw himself forward. He landed with a splattering of mud right against Othelia, sending them both sprawling into the blackness. I had never seen Othelia move so quickly. She was back on her feet in a flash, blinking mud from frightened eyes, and smacking angry jaws. When she could speak again, she turned to Hawkins and a scream came from her throat. "Hawkins," she squealed, "you...you bully. You...you dumped me." She began to cry.

Mother was on her feet then, grunting out comforting words to Othelia and, in the next breath, reprimanding Hawkins. By now, he was up on his own four feet blinking away mud and smacking in satisfaction.

"Don't cry," said Mother to Othelia. "The mud won't hurt you. Why, we love the mud, all of us." Then she turned to Hawkins and her voice lowered. "Don't push," she said sternly. "Your sister was brave enough to be first. You let her take her time in getting into the Hole."

Othelia waded gingerly back to the dry ground. She was still whimpering, but at least the loud wails had stopped. Hawkins never even looked repentant, though it was difficult to see how he looked with him being covered with mud.

Millie and Tillie moved forward to comfort Othelia as soon as her feet left the Hole. They soothed and consoled and said nasty things about Hawkins. They steered her to a dry corner of the yard where straw had been scattered for a bedding-down place.

Hawkins waded out, a grin still on his face. He looked directly at me and muttered one word, "Sissy!"

I hadn't set one foot into the gooey mud in front of me. And Hawkins knew it. I was tempted to turn and hurl myself into the Hole as Hawkins had done to show him that I wasn't a sissy. One close look at the black stuff was enough to change my mind. I felt like hurling myself at Hawkins instead. But one look at his dripping, gooey body changed my mind about that as well. Without a word, I turned and followed my sisters up to the straw bed. As soon as Othelia had been sufficiently consoled, we all curled up together and had ourselves another sleep. None of us felt quite ready for the Mud Hole yet.

Mother roused us later and fed us again. We were glad to eat but, as I reached for the food, I got a mouthful of the gooey mud. I didn't like the taste. I spit it out and tried again. It took about four mouthfuls-and-spits before I was able to begin on my dinner.

The sun had moved lower in the sky and the day was cooling off. As soon as we had finished eating, Mother lunged to her feet. We fell - scattering again. We should have been used to her sudden moves by now but it seemed that she always caught us off guard.

"We should go in," she said, sounding a bit disappointed. "You have been out long enough and soon it will get cool again."

With those words she moved toward the big structure at the end of the yard and I knew that we were going home.

The Cow family was standing at the side of the barn waiting at a great big door.

"It is almost milking time," said Mother in explanation. I didn't understand what milking time was and didn't ask.

The Horse family was at a huge trough dipping and lifting dribbling chins. I watched them as I walked past. Would they decide that they'd had enough of whatever it was, and start moving our way? They didn't.

Just as we were about to enter the small door that

led into our pen I saw something very strange. Many very strange things. In a side yard were a number of shifting, moving, bodies; fat with fuzzy-blanketed sides.

"What's that?" I whispered to Mother, my eyes big with disbelief.

"The Sheep family," answered Mother. She was too far away to call her greeting to our neighbors so she kept right on walking into the shed.

I stopped in my tracks and stared at the funny creatures. They were about as tall as Mother - but very different in build. They had black, skinny faces with floppy ears hanging down almost over their eyes. Their sides were not smooth and bristled like ours. They looked like someone had stuffed them with - with - I didn't know what. I had never seen anything quite like them before.

They talked excitedly back and forth as they chewed. I noticed that they ate the same thing as the giant Cow family. I couldn't stop watching them until I realized that all of my family had entered the warm shed. I, alone, was standing and staring. I took one last look and scrambled into our pen. My mind was full of so many questions that I could hardly wait to talk to Mother.

CHAPTER FIVE
NEIGHBORS

We went to the Hole each day after that. Usually we met the Cow family, the Horse family and, of course, the other members of our Pig family. We heard the Sheep family talking but they were not in the same yard as we were so we really didn't meet them.

Mother was always most anxious to head straight for the Hole. We scrambled along at her side or at her heels, squealing our protests at her fast pace. She would make an effort to slow down for a few steps. Then her eagerness would carry her forward again at a faster clip and we'd be left to scramble after her.

As soon as she greeted her friends she would take us to the straw pile and feed us before going off to the Hole. After eating, we would curl up in the comfort of the dry straw and enjoy the warmth of the sun on our backs. None of us, not even Hawkins, had much interest in the Hole.

One morning I noticed the family of Mrs. Red Sow frolicking in the mud. They seemed to enjoy it. It made me wonder if it might be fun after all, but I quickly dismissed it from my mind and turned over so that the sun would warm my other side.

Mrs. Young Sow had disappeared from our yard. Mother beamed when she was informed that another six piglets had joined us on the farm.

"Are they all well?" she asked Mrs. Red Sow who gave us the news.

"I hear that they are all just fine," answered Mrs. Red Sow.

Mother looked pleased. "I am so happy for her," she bubbled and Mrs. Red Sow seemed to agree. She cast a pleased look at her own squabbling, noisy brood and sighed deeply. "But they grow up so quickly," she said with a hint of sadness in her voice.

Mother nodded, but when she looked at us I saw pleasure rather than sadness in her eyes. I guess she knew that we'd be around for some time to come.

Each day the sun seemed to be a little bit warmer and our yard became a little bit drier. There were even a few spots where the ground was dusty rather than soggy wet. The path where the big Horse family thundered their way sent up little puffs of dust as the big feet hammered against it.

Usually we ignored the barnyard families. We curled up in the straw and toasted our backs as Mother enjoyed the mud with the bigger pigs. If the Horse or Cow family detoured from the trail and came toward the straw to lay in the sun themselves, we scurried away in fright, calling out to Mother to come and rescue us.

Mother would always scurry up from the mud, blinking and grunting as she tried to assure us that we would be just fine as long as we kept out from under the feet of the big animals.

The Horse family didn't come our way often, preferring to catch a few winks as they stood on those four huge feet, heads drooping in drowsiness, eyes shut against the bright sun. But the Cow family often flopped down in the straw as though they had a perfect right to usurp our bed without asking permission.

I watched them from a distance after scampering away with my brothers and sisters. They would lie down with a groan, then stay there contentedly. Their huge jaws continued to work as though they were still eating dinner, although they weren't even lowering their heads to pick up more food.

I always wondered about their pretense but it was Bee-Bee who asked Mother about it.

"Why do they keep chewing when they aren't eating?" she said.

"They eat differently than we do," replied Mother.

Bee-Bee's eyes widened.

"They just sort of chew their food quickly and swallow," continued Mother. "They do that until they have a tummy full, then they lie down somewhere and bring up bits of it to chew it thoroughly."

Bee-Bee made a face.

"Why don't they chew it right the first time?" she asked.

Mother shook her head as though it was beyond her, but then she said with tolerance, "That's the way Cows are. They like to eat quickly until they are full - and then lie down and enjoy it."

"Do you ever do that?" asked Bee-Bee.

"Oh, no," said Mother quickly. "I always enjoy it while I eat."

It seemed the most sensible way to me.

"Well, I wish they wouldn't always take our bed," grumbled Hawkins. For once I found myself in complete agreement with him.

"Oh, it isn't just our bed," Mother informed us. "Man put it there for all of the farmyard animals to use."

That was a surprise to us. We thought the straw bed was for us alone.

"Why?" I asked quickly. "They're big. They don't need it. Why don't they stand up and sleep like - like Horse?"

"They rest better when they lie down," answered Mother.

"Well, why don't they lie down in the Hole, then?" asked Higgins.

Mother shook her head slowly. She seemed to be thinking deeply. "I have never seen them in the Hole," she said at last, "though I really don't know why. I guess, they must just prefer the straw bed."

It didn't seem fair to me - or to any of us - but we were hardly in a position to argue with the Cow family so we took our naps when we could. Whenever the Cow family decided to lie down and chew, we ran squealing to Mother.

One day we were joined by a family as small, and smaller, than ourselves. They came marching on only two feet right onto our straw pile as though they belonged there. They were rather noisy about it, too.

The biggest one, with the colorful tail, led the way, calling out for the rest of them to follow. A slightly smaller one came close at his heels. Behind her some very little ones bobbed and scrambled and tumbled their way. They were so tiny that one could scarcely see them in the dips and hollows of the straw pile but you could certainly hear them.

I had been sleeping with the rest of the family but the noise woke me. I opened one eye lazily to see what the racket was all about. The newcomers surprised me so that I opened both eyes and watched as they approached.

I felt no fear. Even though there seemed to be a multitude of them, they were small and didn't look like they could possibly cause one bodily harm.

"There should be something in here worth scratching for," the biggest one was saying. The second one answered with a pleased voice, "Thank you. Thank you." She immediately began to scratch.

The little ones arrived from all directions, flocking around the bigger one, peeping and chirping and asking for reassurance.

She answered them as she scratched. Her voice was filled with love for her babies and excitement over finding whatever she was looking for.

Some of the tiny young ones began to scratch with their little feet. I don't know if they found anything but they called excitedly and made a lot of

noise. A few of them pecked away at the straw.

I wiggled around slightly so I could get a better look at them, hoping not to rouse my sleeping brothers and sisters. Sometimes they got awfully riled up when someone disturbed their rest.

I managed to wiggle just enough to lift my head and watch the strange actions. The biggest fellow strutted, then called, then scratched, by turn. The second biggest murmured her excited thanks and moved in to scratch beside him. He looked very pleased with himself as he led her closer and closer to where we slept in the straw. With each step the two of them made, the little ones clamored and clustered around them, trying their hardest to get their little feet to scratch up something for their dinner as well.

I was fascinated by it all and I couldn't resist hoisting myself up for a better look. My movement awakened Hawkins. With an angry protest he heaved himself up to a sitting position and yelled at me to be still and stop shoving his face in the straw.

That, of course, was unfair. I hadn't shoved him, at least not much. His protest brought Othelia up. With one movement the half-buried pile of piglets came screaming up from our bed, angry voices scolding one another and straw flying in all directions.

Say, you should have seen those new creatures! I would never have guessed that they could move so quickly. The biggest one let out a squawk that even startled me. And the second biggest one was almost as loud. The little ones cried out in alarm and scattered in all directions. Feathers flew along with the straw, and voices screamed, "Run for your lives! Giants! Run for your lives!"

I had never witnessed anything so funny and I couldn't help but laugh at the sight. Hawkins was still not wide enough awake to appreciate the humor of the whole affair.

What's so funny about wakin' a guy up from a sound sleep?" he grumbled.

I laughed even harder. "They called us giants," I informed him.

"So?" demanded Othelia, shaking straw from her ears.

"They thought that we were giants," I said again. "They flew out of here like we were... were..."

Bee-Bee blinked at the bright sunshine and then began to grin. Across the barnyard the frightened family was still screaming and calling. The biggest one yelled at us to keep our distance or else. The second biggest one gathered the babies together and counted them over and over to be sure that they were all there.

"They thought that we were giants?" grinned Bee-Bee. Then she asked in a more sober voice, "Why?"

"Well, I...I...I guess we're growing up," I said and pushed myself up from the straw to stand to my full height. It felt good to be considered a giant.

Then Hawkins stood up, swelled up his chest and pushed up on tiptoe until he towered over me. "Yeah," he said with a grin of his own. "We're growing up."

He looked down at me as if he was the only one who had done any significant growing. I angrily pushed my way past him. "The big show-off," I thought to myself. He had taken all the fun out of the day again.

I started toward the Hole to find Mother. I was curious about the new visitors who had considered us - us piglets - to be giants in the straw. I wanted to ask Mother who they were and where they came from. I hoped that they lived close enough so that they would come back again. It was rather nice to be considered a giant after living with monster Cows and Horses. I swaggered just a bit as I headed for the Hole. Then I looked back over my shoulder and spotted the strange new family at the barnyard fence. The big one was on the top rail. He yelled at us one last time but he was too far away for me to understand the insult. The second biggest one was still nervously shepherding all of the little ones. She clucked and called and coaxed them to make haste in ducking their way under the barnyard fence to put a safe distance between themselves and the "giants." I grinned again and hurried off to the Mud Hole. After the excitement had died down, my sisters and brothers had buried themselves in the straw again and continued their afternoon nap.

CHAPTER SIX
EATING OUT

We weren't very old when we became interested in what Mother was eating. She seemed to enjoy it so much and it did smell temptingly good. Hawkins, still being the biggest of us, was the first one to try something from her trough. I don't know how he managed to reach it, but he did. I guess his legs were a bit longer than mine. I had tried my hardest and still was unable to stretch quite far enough to reach the food.

But Hawkins did! He came out smacking his lips and looking like he was the ruler of the universe. So smug and pleased with himself, he was. It made me even more determined to stretch my way up into that trough, too.

A few days passed by and I still wasn't big enough to reach. Hawkins kept stealing a bite here and a bite there and grinning from ear to ear as he smacked and chomped. It really upset me but there wasn't much I could do about it.

One day as we cuddled up in the straw bed and Mother rolled contentedly in the Hole, Man came to the yard and dumped a whole pail full of fine-smelling stuff into the outside trough for the family of Mrs. Red Sow.

My stomach rumbled with the desire to join them. Yet, as I watched, it knotted up in fright too.

I had never seen such pushing and shoving as went on at that trough. It was plenty long enough for eight middle-sized pigs, but you would have thought that there was room for only one. They pushed and shoved and squealed and screamed and fought for every mouthful they took.

I trembled as I watched them and then I thought of something. The outside trough from which they ate was much lower than the one inside where Mother usually took her dinner.

"I'll bet I could reach it," I whispered to myself.

Once the idea had come to me I knew that I'd have to check it out. My eyes went back to the teeming mass of piggery. Surely I would be trampled to death if I even tried such a foolhardy thing.

My stomach rumbled again and the smell of the food wafted toward me on the soft afternoon breeze. I saw Hawkins' snout twitch in his sleep. I was sure that he smelled the delicious odor as well and probably assumed that he was only dreaming it.

That twitching snout made up my mind for me. I would get a bit of that dinner - or die in the attempt. If I didn't, Hawkins would discover it first and lord it over me again.

Carefully, oh so carefully, I wiggled my way out of the straw away from the other family members. At one point Hawkins stirred, smacked his lips and lifted his snout slightly for another sniff. I was sure that he was going to awaken and beat me to the trough. I held my breath, ready to make a dash should he so much as lift his head. But he only smacked a few more times, then buried his head deeper in the soft straw. I breathed easier and pushed myself carefully away from Bee-Bee.

As soon as I was on my feet, I started for the food. At the rate those pig fellows were eating, I was afraid I would get there too late and would be trampled to death for nothing.

They didn't even seem to notice me as I rushed up to join them. That was both good and bad. Good, because no one turned to me and said that I had no business trying to horn in on their dinner. Bad, because they paid no attention whatever to where they were putting their sharp hoofs or shoving their frantic bodies.

For just a moment I stood there and tried to pick an opening. One came when one big fellow, with a thrust of his nose, sent a brother floundering to the ground. Before the fallen one could regain his feet, I flung myself directly forward toward the trough.

But the opening closed before I could even take advantage of it. Another member of the family quickly thrust herself into the vacated spot. I squealed my anger and disappointment and quickly dashed away before the kicking, striking feet had a chance to reach me.

I had to draw back and look for an opening again. It seemed to take forever before another one appeared. I was sure that every morsel of food would be devoured before I could get near the trough.

At last a small rift appeared between two shuffling pigs and I ran for it, almost getting myself squeezed to death for my effort.

As if by a miracle, I was able to grab one mouthful before I had to quickly duck out again.

It was just as I had thought. The food, whatever it was, was delicious.

I backed off a few steps and stood chewing and chomping, smacking my jaws and enjoying myself as I never had before. Now I knew why Hawkins looked so smug.

As soon as I had swallowed the last taste of the food, I was ready for more. I was a bit bolder now and didn't wait as long as I should have to find the proper opening. As soon as just a small opportunity presented itself, I dashed forward.

Two big bodies quickly closed the gap and I felt myself being lifted up and then falling. Above my head I could see shifting bodies and thousands - or so it seemed - of sharp, scrambling feet. I ducked one foot, then two. A third one scraped against my side and a fourth almost pinned one of my ears to the ground.

With a frightened squeal I fought my way out from under the wriggling bodies and gasped for breath. I had nearly gotten myself trampled to death.

After withdrawing a few feet, I stood trembling. I had no business trying to share their meal. They were much bigger than I and had no intention of welcoming me to their feast.

I shook my head and determined to go back to my

safe, straw bed when a waft of breeze brought me the odor of the dinner again.

I couldn't resist it. I had to try one more time.

This time I picked my spot with more care. It didn't take long for an opening to appear. As soon as it did, I sprang forward, hurling myself at the trough intending to grab another big bite and then withdraw. Just as I went to heave myself up to grab that bite, someone else decided to give me a boost. At least that's the way it felt. Suddenly I felt myself being lifted in the air and flying, all four feet turned upward.

I landed with a thump. For a minute the wind was knocked out of me and I had no idea where I was. When I finally came to my senses, I realized that I was in the feeding trough.

Panic swept through me. I wasn't sure if that squealing, fighting family was smart enough to realize that I wasn't intended to be part of their dinner.

I scrambled to my feet, screaming loudly that I was Pig, their brother. And that I wasn't a part of the menu at all.

For just a moment I saw a few looks of surprise and a bit of hesitation. Then they charged right in to eating the main course again.

I screamed for Mother then. I was sure that if one of those hungry mouths should happen to get hold of me, they wouldn't even slow down.

I didn't even think about grabbing a few mouthfuls myself. I was much too concerned with staying away from hungry jaws. I don't suppose they would really have eaten me - but, at the time, I was scared to death and not taking any chances.

"Mother," I screamed again. "Mother! Save me."

I don't know how such a big, lumbering pig made it from the Hole to the trough so quickly. But there she was, tossing her head and telling the whole litter to back off. She fought her way through them, flinging bodies this way and that when they didn't move fast enough.

They weren't very happy with the rude interruption and squealed back at her angrily. In the distance I heard Mrs. Red Sow call a warning to Mother to be careful how she handled her family.

Mother didn't seem to hear her. She just pushed her way in until she found me. Then she grunted excitedly asking where I was hurt and what I was doing in the feeding trough.

I managed to get up onto four shaky legs and tried to scramble over the edge. It took help from Mother's snout for me to make it. At last I landed on the ground with a thump and Mother nosed me anxiously to make sure I was all right.

As soon as she was convinced that I wasn't hurt she grunted an apology to the litter and urged me away from the trough.

"What happened?" she asked as she gently nudged me toward the straw pile. All of my bothers and sisters were gathered wide-eyed, watching the commotion.

"I...I was just...just hungry," I responded sheepishly.

"Hungry? Then why didn't you call me?"

"Well,...well, I...The food in the trough smelled so good and...and...I can never reach it from your trough and...and Hawkins always..."

"I see," said Mother. From the tone of her voice I felt that maybe she did.

We walked slowly in silence. Things had quieted down now. In the distance I could hear the bigger pigs still fighting over their dinner. I really wasn't tempted to go back and force my way in again.

At last Mother spoke. "You are really too small to be fighting your way at a feeding trough," she said gently. "If you are so determined to try out the food, you must eat from my trough. I'll give you a boost - if you need one. But it won't be long until you'll be able to reach it on your own."

I felt much better then. I hadn't even needed to explain about Hawkins. How he was always bigger, and first, about everything.

"You needn't be in too big a hurry," continued Mother. "All things happen in their own good time. You'll see."

We reached the straw bed and Mother nosed her way around and then lowered herself into the softness. Immediately we all rushed forward.

I was the first one there. When I found my position I held on tightly as the kicking and squealing litter jockeyed for position.

I closed my eyes and braced myself for the pushing that I knew would come.

"We really aren't much different from the ones

at the trough," I admitted to myself. Then I grinned. I might be pushed and shoved around at my own dinner table - but at least I wasn't worried about being trampled to death. And then a new thought came. "And I am growing - even I can see that. Now that Mother is going to help me reach her feeding trough, who knows? I might catch up to Hawkins yet."

Mother and the other larger pigs often rooted around in the ground and came up with satisfied looks and smacking jaws.

"What are they doing?" murmured Othelia.

I shrugged my shoulders. I wasn't sure, but whatever it was, they seemed to be finding something to eat.

It was Bee-Bee who pushed forward and dared to ask Mother.

"What are you doing?"

"Eating," Mother said simply.

"Eating? What?" continued Bee-Bee.

"There are all sorts of good things in the ground," said Mother. From the way that she was smacking, we knew that she was right.

"How do you find it?' asked Othelia.

"Just shove your nose in and give a push this way and that," said Mother.

"How do you know what is good?" asked Bee-Bee.

"If it tastes good - eat it," responded Mother.

Othelia looked hesitant.

I cast a glance toward Hawkins. Surely he would be the first to try it just to outdo me. I quickly

thrust my nose at the ground with as much effort as I could put behind it.

Whump! For a minute I saw stars.

"No, No. Not like that," said Mother. "You must push and wiggle and lift. Like this. Watch!"

I wished that she had explained more thoroughly in the first place.

Mother gave us a demonstration of how to thrust one's nose into the warm ground and wiggle and thrust until one exposed something that was good to eat.

It took a while for us to catch on. Sure enough, it was Hawkins who was successful first. He wasn't modest about it either.

"Look!" he cried for everyone to see. "Look! I did it. I did it. I got my nose right into the ground."

Hawkins stood with little bits of black earth slowly dribbling down the sides of his nose. He didn't have a thing in his mouth - which was, after all, the purpose of the whole exercise. But he seemed to have forgotten that.

"Good!" said Mother, very pleased with the effort of Hawkins. "Now the rest of you try it."

We pushed and wriggled and shoved at the earth with our small snouts. One by one we raised our heads to squeal when we accomplished the task. The second part of the lesson involved actually coming up with something worth chewing. After a few unsuccessful efforts, we were able to do that as well. I guess each one of us felt very smug and grown-up.

CHAPTER SEVEN
THE HOLE

I don't know exactly when the idea came to me that it might be fun in the mud. I guess it came gradually. Perhaps it was because of the older litter of pigs. They seemed to have a good time whenever they entered the Hole - much to the annoyance of the older ones who just liked to recline with eyes closed, shifting from one side to another as they felt the need.

The younger ones couldn't stay in one position for long. They pushed and jostled and purposely bumped one another. The whole procedure looked like it had possibilities.

"Do you think we should try it?" I asked Othelia one day as we stood watching the shoving. We were not spending as much of our time curled up in the straw now. We were beginning to feel just a trifle bored.

She looked at me with a "Humph," and moved off toward the straw again. Bee-Bee quickly took her place beside me.

"Let's," she said in an excited whisper.

That was all I needed.

With loud squeals we dashed toward the Hole

and flung ourselves in with a mighty splash. Mud flew everywhere. Angry protests greeted our arrival. Even Mother lifted herself to a sitting position, removing the mud from her face with a shake of her huge head. Her eyes blinked in the brightness of the sunshine.

"You are welcome to come in," she said with her usual patience, "but learn to do it more slowly."

But Bee-Bee and I were laughing so hard that we hardly heard her.

Mother lowered herself once again and closed her eyes against the day's brightness. Only her ear showed that she was a living thing. The big ear that was exposed flicked in annoyance once in a while at some bothering fly.

I nodded my head toward the Hole's edge and Bee-Bee understood my meaning. We scrambled our way to the dry ground and braced ourselves for another fling into the mud. This time I counted, "One, Two, Three," and we ran at the Hole again.

Again the other pigs complained. Mrs. Red Sow lumbered to her feet and moved further into the Hole, gently complaining that there would be "no peace and quiet now with so many youngsters underfoot."

Mother didn't seem to hear the protests. Her eyes blinked open and closed again. She seemed to prepare herself for constant interruptions. A deep sigh shook her large frame. I could see the pile of mud lift and fall as she sucked in her breath. She snuggled down into the coolness of the mud and closed her eyes as though hoping to be able to shut out our wild antics.

I guess the others heard our shouts and laughter for it wasn't long before Higgins stood at the edge of the Hole watching us. Soon Millie and Tillie were there too.

Higgins was the first of the three to hurl himself in. He was little but he was wiry, and the force of his small body hitting the mud sent Bee-Bee and me floundering in it again. All three of us came up black and muddy and laughing.

Millie, or Tillie, I wasn't sure which, couldn't resist the fun and threw herself in to join us. We all wallowed and scrambled and rose to our feet only to slip and be buried in the mud again. It was fun. We laughed so hard that we could scarcely stand long enough to get back to solid ground at the edge again.

The older litter grumbled a good deal, complaining about the "kids" and their "crazy play." They moved off some distance and buried their noses in the mud, trying hard to ignore us completely.

By now Othelia couldn't resist the Hole, but she made the mistake of entering gingerly, lifting each foot high in the air as though holding up her skirts so she wouldn't get them dirty. It looked so silly to the rest of us that we couldn't keep from making a dash at her and completely burying her in the goo. At first she was angry, but soon she discovered that it was fun and she joined in our play.

I don't know where Hawkins had been. Probably looking for food somewhere. Though he still joined us for dinner whenever Mother fed us, he had already declared that there were all kinds of good things to eat just waiting to be found. He often came in bragging and smacking about something that he had discovered. As I looked around the circle of mud-players, I figured that he was likely off "piggin' out" somewhere again.

I didn't care. At least I tried to tell myself that I didn't care. I was a little upset, though. I didn't like to think of Hawkins enjoying something that I wasn't enjoying. Nor did I like to think of him growing fast because of all of his eating. He was still bigger than I was. Down deep inside I knew that might mean that he would be chosen by Girl for her project, whatever it was.

I turned my attention back to the Hole. Bee-Bee had just flung herself in and Higgins followed, landing almost on top of her. It caused her to flounder in the sticky black substance.

Bee-Bee took it good-naturedly. Her head came up and she blinked her eyes and gulped for air a couple times but then she grinned.

Hawkins soon appeared. Sure enough he was looking pleased with himself and smacking away. I was sure he had found something new to eat and I also knew that we would hear his boasting. His eyes met mine and he grinned. I turned away from him before he could see that I was angry and envious. He must have turned to Othelia then. He knew that her curiousity would have her asking.

"What've you got?" she asked as Hawkins knew she would. Though I tried not to let my interest show, I stayed close enough to hear his answer.

"I don't know - but it sure is good."

"Where'd you get it?" asked Othelia. I turned just enough to see her eyes scanning the yard hungrily.

"There was only one," boasted Hawkins, "an' I got it."

"One what?" interruped Bee-Bee, joining us.

Hawkins smacked even more. He grinned and looked from one of us to the other.

"Where'd you find it?" asked Othelia again, insistently.

"Over there," said Hawkins with a careless toss of his head. "In the corner by the straw pile, tucked in behind those boards. I had to really work to get at it. Nearly broke my snout..."

But Hawkins didn't get to finish. From the corner that he had spoken of came such a squawking and screaming as I had never heard before in my life. Right at us came a half-running, half-flying creature with arms outstretched and long neck bobbing. He hissed out such awful threats and name-calling that it made our bristles stand on end.

I wasn't waiting to see what would happen next. I threw myself into the Hole as close to Mother as I could get, terror filling my whole being. I was sure that the angry screamer was out to get us all.

One after the other, my frightened brothers and sisters threw themselves in the Hole behind me and we all struggled to get to Mother as quickly as we could. We were sure that our very lives depended upon it.

That is, all but Hawkins. He just stood there stupidly, enjoying whatever it was that he was eating. He must have had it all down by then, but he still stood smacking his lips with deep satisfaction.

Just as I reached Mother's side, she heaved herself upward - as did every other pig in the Hole. Nervous grunts filled the air and shifting bodies made the mud lift and fall.

"What is it? What is it?" everyone was saying in unison.

Mother blinked her eyes against the sun, opened them fully and took in the screaming creatures on the shore and the innocent-looking Hawkins who didn't have sense enough to get out of their way.

I guess Mother feared for Hawkins, even if he was too dumb to fear for himself. She lunged to her feet and, with excited grunts, made quickly for the shore.

Another angry creature had joined the first and it was stretching its long neck out toward Hawkins too, screaming and screeching and hissing threats. Hawkins just stood there blinking.

"What is it? What's the matter?" called Mother before she even reached firm ground.

The noise increased. Even though I was a safe distance away from the commotion, I lowered myself into the mud hoping to hide completely from the fracas.

"Him!" shouted the biggest of the pair. "He did it! He did it!" The second one joined in, circling closer and closer to Hawkins and screaming together, "He did it! He did it!"

At that point I realized that Hawkins had managed to get himself into trouble. For just one tiny moment I felt rather smug about the fact. Then I looked back at the angry pair and I hoped that Mother would get there in time to save my brother.

"He did what?" asked Mother as she struggled from the mud and heaved herself up to her full height on the shore. Even though she looked big beside the angry pair, they did not back down one inch. Mother placed herself between their pointing, accusing beaks and Hawkins.

"Our egg," one of them screamed viciously. "Our egg. He stole it. He stole our egg."

The noise became almost unbearable. One of the angry pair reached out and gave Hawkins a peck with a sharp beak. Hawkins cried out in pain and Mother stepped forward.

As soon as the din died down enough for Mother to be heard, she turned to Hawkins.

"Is this true?" she asked. I could detect a tremor in her voice. I was sure that Mother was hoping that Hawkins could draw himself up to his full height and deny the charge. But Hawkins only shook his head stupidly and blinked his eyes.

"I dunno," he shrugged, then made the mistake of smacking his chops thinking of the tasty morsel he had just devoured.

"He did! He did it!" screamed the pair of fluttering fowl.

Mother waited until they settled down a bit. "Hawkins, did you steal their egg?" she asked directly.

He shrugged again - but this time he knew enough

not to smack his lips. "I...I ate...something," he admitted, "but I don't know what it was."

He stood there looking as innocent as it is possible for a too-big-for-his-age, overly-fat, smug-looking pig to look innocent.

"See!" screamed the angry pair to Mother. "See! He admits it."

They whirled again on Hawkins. "You thief!" they screamed. "You...you thoughtless, miserable thief."

One of them moved forward as if to give Hawkins a good lesson in manners. The other cried out, more angry than ever, "I laid it just this morning! Just this morning! And you...you..."

She broke off, too angry to talk.

Mother stepped forward again and placed herself between Hawkins and the hissing barnyard fowl.

"I...I am dreadfully sorry about your egg," Mother began. "I don't blame you one bit for being terribly angry. I would be angry too, if it had happened to me. But, well, it is partly my fault. I hadn't realized that it is already nest building time and I...I had completely forgotten to tell the children to be careful about the eggs."

The two still shrieked but gradually the clamor subsided.

"Hawkins," said Mother in her firmest voice, "you must apologize to Geese for stealing from their nest. You must never touch their eggs again. Do you understand?"

Hawkins nodded his head. Secretly I wondered if he would really be able to keep his promise if he ever came across another tasty goose egg.

"Now—apologize," urged Mother.

"I...I..." stammered Hawkins. He never had been any good at apologies.

Mother prodded him with her long snout.

"I'm sorry," said Hawkins quickly.

"And you will not touch their eggs again," urged Mother.

Hawkins looked a bit reluctant to voice those words.

Mother prodded him again.

"I'll...I'll not eat your eggs," Hawkins blurted at last.

"You'll not have the chance," hissed the larger of the two geese. "We'll be taking our nest elsewhere. We'll not take a chance with a...with a marauding, thieving pig. You can be sure of that."

The smaller one added her voice to that of her mate.

"Yes. You can be sure of that. No more thieving pigs stealing from our nest. We're moving to the sheep pen. The sheep have better manners. They never steal from our nest."

With hisses and honks they moved away, tossing heads held high on long, jerking necks. They were still terribly angry.

As soon as they had ducked and squirmed their way under the gate separating us from the sheep pen, Hawkins smacked his lips again. I knew that he was thinking of how good that egg had tasted and feeling sorry that the sheep pen would now house the nest of tempting goodies. I followed

Hawkins' eyes as they looked longingly through the fence and into the sheep pen. I wondered if he was figuring whether there was a way that he could squeeze under that fence.

Mother must have read his thoughts too. She turned to him and spoke sternly, "Hawkins, don't you dare ever steal from their nest again. Do you hear me? We must live at peace with our neighbors. One hardly does that by robbing nests."

Hawkins nodded in agreement but I saw the disappointment in his eyes.

I turned back to my brother and sisters and we began playing in the mud again. We all wanted to have as much fun as we could before Hawkins plunged into the Hole and spoiled it for us.

CHAPTER EIGHT

DISCOVERY

"You know," Hawkins said to me one day, "I could root my way right out of this yard."

I thought it was just another of his boasts. But if there was a chance that he really could do as he claimed, I wanted to get in on it. I had been eyeing the big garden patch just beyond our fence.

"Humph!" I responded, hoping to make him prove himself. "How do you plan to do that?"

"Right under that gate."

I was sure that there had been a time when any of us would have been able to slip under the gate. At that time we wanted to stay close to our mother. Certainly she would not have fitted under the gate so we had not even thought about it.

Now we were older and bigger. We didn't depend on her as much anymore. But now we were also too big to slip out under the gate.

"Goose did it. Remember?"

How well I remembered the goose family leaving by sitting down in the dust and squirming their way under the fence. They had never been back to our yard again. Occasionally we heard them honking and calling to one another in the sheep pen next door. The sheep had vacated that pen now. Mother said that Man had moved them to a pasture where there was green grass for them to eat. The Cow and Horse families often left our yard for feeding elsewhere as well.

I missed all of the families gone from our barnyard. It didn't seem fair that they got to go to new places to dine and we had to stay right where we were. Our yard had been rooted until there were very few new places to turn up sod. Our big Mud Hole was getting smaller and smaller as the summer passed while we were all getting bigger and bigger.

We couldn't claim to be hungry. Man saw to that. As we grew, so did the food in the feeding trough. We could all reach it now. That is, all but the youngest litter in the yard. Mrs. Young Sow had joined us with her six. In fact they had taken over our soft bed in the straw pile. Not that we minded. It made us feel grown-up to yield to someone younger and smaller than we were.

I guess we were rather restless. Or bored. Or something. Anyway, Hawkins was always throwing out new challenges. I looked at him now and dared him to follow through with his boast.

"Let's see you do it," I flung at him.

"You don't think I can, do you?" he grunted back.

I tossed my head so that my ears flopped and frightened off the two flies that had been picking in the dirt left from my last mud bath. "No," I said simply, "I don't."

He didn't even answer me, just headed straight for the gate and lowered his snout to the ground. I think he was surprised at the hardness of the beaten path. It had been walked on for so many years that it was packed solid. He kept on pushing and wriggling his nose but I could see that he wasn't going to get anywhere.

In disgust I turned and walked away from him. It looked like we were all destined to root up ground that had been turned again and again.

I could hear Hawkins behind me as he pushed and shoved at the hard ground near the gate.

Just before I got out of earshot I turned and called out to him rather angrily, "Oh, give it up, will you? You can't make a dent in that packed earth."

I headed for the Hole where the girls and Higgins had joined Mother for a mud bath.

"I hope it rains soon," Mrs. Red Sow was saying as I neared the Hole. "We are getting down to where one can scarcely get a good bath anymore."

"Yes," Mother agreed, "we do need rain. When the Horse and Cow families come through the yard, I almost choke from the dust they stir up."

I had seen it rain a few times but I didn't care much for it. I sure couldn't see why Mother and Mrs. Red Sow were wishing for it to happen again.

"And the straw," said Mrs. Young Sow, "It is getting so dusty that my poor piglets are wheezing."

"We need a good rain all right," said Mrs. Red Sow.

I cast a glance toward the sky and then waded

into the Hole. It was shallow. It hardly even covered my body as I lay down in it. I could remember when my sisters, brothers and I wouldn't have dared venture into the spot where I lay now. It had been left for the big pigs.

That very night a wind began to blow and soon a dark cloud had covered the moon. We were sleeping outside now that we had grown a good deal. We still found a spot where we could all lie down together. Mother always fed us just before we closed our eyes in sleep. She didn't leave us during the night. I wouldn't have admitted it to anyone but I always enjoyed the night time, curled up tightly with Mother and the rest of the litter. It gave me a safe and cared-for feeling.

I wasn't sure just what awakened me—the whining wind or Mother's restless stirring but suddenly I was awake, knowing something was different about the night.

I looked up where the stars usually clustered overhead and I couldn't locate a single star. Alarm filled me. I wondered what had happened to all of them when Mother stirred again. I saw her lift her head and sniff the air then she clambered to her feet, rousing all seven of us with her action.

"It's going to rain," she said when we whined our protest. "We should go to the pen in the shed."

It surprised me. We had been out in showers before but nothing had happened to us.

Even as Mother spoke she was moving toward our old home in the shed.

We had taken only a few steps when the first big

drops began to fall. They splattered around us with whipping force, driven by the wind that was blowing in from the north.

By the time we reached our door we were being pelted. We ran the last few steps and all tried to duck in out of the cold rain at the same time. There wasn't enough room, of course. Hawkins and I got stuck in the doorway together before we were able to wriggle ourselves free.

After we had quieted ourselves and curled up against Mother in the dryness of the barn, we could still hear the drumming of the rain. It pounded on our tin roof with a deafening hammering. I hated the sound but above the din I could hear Mother's contented grunts. "Good," she said as if to herself, "more water for the Hole."

I agreed that it was good to have more water for the Hole, but I did wish that there was a quieter way to do it.

The rain continued to fall all the next day. It had settled down now to a gentler rain, falling steadily but without the strong wind to drive it so hard. Mother ventured in and out during the day. I went outside twice but I really didn't like the feel of the cold water on my back and running down the sides of my face. I didn't stay out long before I would duck back in to warm up in our straw bed again.

It was still raining the next day. I began to wonder if it would ever stop. Mother and her friends seemed pleased with the rain and its promise of filling the Hole again.

"Isn't this wonderful?" said Mrs. Red Sow.

"The Hole will fill and things will grow in the yard again. We will have fresh shoots and roots to eat."

"Yes," agreed Mother, looking pleased, "and we won't choke on the dust anymore."

"And my babies won't be bothered with the dust from the straw," added Mrs. Young Sow.

I was glad that they were all happy about the rain, but secretly I hoped that it would end quickly so we could enjoy all of the good things that it was supposed to bring.

At last the clouds rolled away and the sun came out. Boy, it was good to get back out into the yard.

I couldn't believe the changes that the rain had made. The Hole was filled to overflowing. Not only did we have a good supply of mud but there was even extra water, much too deep for pigs my size. The middle of the Hole was even too deep for Mother.

I was disappointed that there were no green things like the older pigs had promised. I voiced my feelings to Mother.

"Oh, you must be patient," she informed me. "It takes time for things to grow. But they will, just you wait and see."

I wandered off, muttering to myself when I spied Hawkins. There he was right beside the gate, his nose buried deeply in the mud of the path. He was still determined to find his way under.

I perked up with sudden interest and cast a glance over my shoulder to see if Mother might be watching. She was much too busy enjoying the new bath to be bothered with the doings of Hawkins.

I walked slowly toward him, pretending not to notice what was going on.

"What are you doing?" I asked as I drew near. "Looking for shoots or roots? Mother says they will take time to grow."

Hawkins didn't even stop to answer me. He just kept right on digging. I could see that he was beginning to make a little bit of headway.

"You think you're going to dig your way out?" I asked with sarcasm edging my voice.

"You'd be smarter to save your breath for digging," answered Hawkins with a sneer and went on with his work.

I had never thought about teaming up with Hawkins before. Suddenly I realized that he was right. Without further comment I shouldered up beside him and put my snout to the ground. It was surprising what the two of us could accomplish together. It wasn't long until we had a fairly good-sized hole under the gate.

I decided that it was time to see if we could wriggle our way out.

"Let me try it," I urged, pushing against Hawkins. "I'm smaller. Let me see if it's big enough for me to fit."

But Hawkins pushed me aside. "Sure," he said, " you'd go ahead and squeeze your way out and leave me to do the rest of the work myself. Nothing doing. You keep digging until it's big enough for either of us."

I didn't say any more. Reluctantly I went back to

work. Hawkins wouldn't let me get near the hole under the gate until he was sure that it was big enough for him to slip through.

As usual, he went first. I followed, trying to push past him to see what there was to be discovered.

We were in a new yard. Several of the barnyard fowl were strolling here and there, with little ones close behind the big ones. Cocks crowed, gobblers gobbled, geese honked and ducks quacked. Neither Hawkins nor I paid the least bit of attention to them. What we did spot almost immediately were feeding troughs and dishes. I guess they belonged to the fowl. At least that is what they told us the minute we got near them.

"That's our food," screamed one big turkey gobbler. "You have your own. Leave ours alone. Leave it! Do you hear me?"

A gander joined in. He made almost as much noise as the pair of geese had made when Hawkins stole their egg. Then a rooster began to shout at us, scrambling to the top of a near-by post with a great whirl of feed and feathers. I thought that he had scattered more of his food than we were likely to consume.

"It's ours! It's ours," he screamed at us. "Leave it alone! Leave it alone."

We paid no attention to all of the squawking and squabbling and went right on raiding one trough after the other.

I was feeling quite smug and independent when there was a new commotion in the yard. I had never heard such a noise in all of my life and I was smart enough to check to see where it was coming from.

The animal that was making all of the fuss was bigger than we were. He was running directly toward us issuing threats and demanding that we vacate the premises. I knew without being told that we were facing the farm dog and he was very angry with two errant young piglets. Hawkins and I did the only sensible thing to do. We swung around, stuck our curly tails in the air and ran for all we were worth.

CHAPTER NINE
REX

I thought that we got a fairly good start as we whirled away from the feeding troughs and bounded out of the yard but our short legs were no match for the long legs of Dog.

If we had been smart, we would have squeezed back under the gate again and looked for Mother. Neither of us thought about that until it was too late.

Instead, we ran in the opposite direction simply because we could see no close fence to impede our progress.

I knew that the farm garden was off in that direction. It had been my intention to go there just as quickly as I had emptied the feeding troughs in the fowl yard. Now I saw the garden as more than a place to get a delicious dinner. It seemed like a fine place to hide. Because of the tall plants and the heavy foliage, I was sure that one small pig could plunge into the growth and be completely hidden from one angry dog.

I don't know what Hawkins was thinking but I noticed, even as I scurried for safety, that he was going in the same direction. I figured that he must be heading for the same place that I was.

Perhaps Dog knew about our plans or about the garden. Although my legs moved just as fast as I could make them go, Dog was able to catch up before we had a chance to duck under the leaves of the rhubarb or into the patch of potatoes.

With a nip to my shoulder he shouted at me to turn. Without hesitation, I turned. I was in no position to argue my case with Dog.

Faster and faster I ran, squealing for Mother and wishing with all of my heart that I'd had the good sense to stay in my own yard.

As I ran it took me a few minutes to realize that I had been left on my own while Dog went after Hawkins. I knew from his outraged cries that it was Hawkins' turn to be nipped. I quickly sized up the situation and altered my course for open ground again.

I don't know why I still wasn't smart enough to head back for the pen, but I wasn't. While Dog busied himself with Hawkins, I made a dash for the farm lane.

Immediately Dog was back at my side again, shouting at me to turn back as he nipped at my heels. I squealed as though I were being put through torture and turned the way Dog directed.

In the meantime Hawkins had made a dash for freedom and Dog had to desert me again to go in hot pursuit.

That was when I realized that two against one gave us a bit of an edge. Perhaps Hawkins realized it at the same time. Whenever Dog would go for

Hawkins, I would race further away from where I knew I should be. Whenever Dog came after me, Hawkins pushed his way a little further down the lane.

Ahead of us was the open end of a culvert. We didn't know what it was or what it was used for, but we both spied it at the same time. We raced toward it, seeing it as safety from the nips of the angry dog.

We nearly made a deadly mistake. As usual we both wanted to be first and we tried to enter the culvert together.

There wasn't enough room for us to enter the opening at the same time. For one sickening moment I envisioned us both stuck in the entrance with Dog angrily nipping at our exposed exterior as we squealed and fought to unstick ourselves and spring to safety.

It almost happened that way, too, but Hawkins reached the opening just ahead of me. After one frightening moment, he was able to push his way past me and I slid in behind him. At my heels Dog gave one more angry nip and I squealed again in anger and pain.

We pushed deeper into the dark interior. Underneath us we could feel wetness but water did not bother us nearly as much as the angry Dog. It was Dog that had us shivering with worry. We could hear his barking at the entrance and see his long nose poke its way in again and again.

"Come out of there," he demanded. "You come out. I'm to keep you in your own yard. You get out

here. Do you hear me? Come on out and go back where you belong."

It took several minutes to assure ourselves that he really couldn't come in after us. As he barked and scolded, we continued to shiver. Then we realized that we were safe. At least we were out of his reach.

"He..he can't get us here," shivered Hawkins and I pressed up against him, glad for his presence. I shivered too. "No, he can't reach us here."

Dog kept right on barking and scolding and we kept right on shivering. Then we heard another voice.

"What is it, boy? Have you cornered something?"

It was the voice of Girl and I thought of bursting out and giving myself up. Somehow I was confident that she would protect me from Dog but Hawkins didn't seem to have that assurance.

"Keep quiet," he whispered with fear edging his voice. "Don't move." So I didn't.

"What is it?" I heard her ask again. Then she went on with a worried voice. "You haven't trapped a skunk under there, have you?"

Dog told her it was some of the barnyard pigs but she didn't seem to understand.

"If it's a skunk," she went on, "you don't want to be making it angry. You could get yourself into a lot of trouble. C'mon. Let's get back to the house."

Dog still objected but I guess Girl won out. I could hear Dog being led away under protest.

Soon things got deathly quiet. Hawkins and I

were both still panting from our run and our hearts were still thumping within our chests. I wondered how long it would take before I would be breathing normally again.

I longed to lie down and rest my tired body but the water trickling through the culvert hardly seemed like a good place to sleep.

Soon we both began to shiver again but this time it was from the cold rather than our fear.

"It's...it's cold in here," sniffled Hawkins.

"I...I know," I answered and pressed up against him for warmth.

"How long do you think we'll have to stay here?" snuffled Hawkins.

"I...I don't know. Until Dog goes to sleep, I guess."

"That will be...will be too long," said Hawkins and he sneezed a noisy sneeze.

"Be quiet," I said crossly. "He'll hear you and come back."

"I can't help it," argued Hawkins and he sneezed again.

We huddled together. The culvert was getting colder and darker.

"Do you think we dare go out now?" sniffed Hawkins.

I wasn't sure. I didn't want to come face to face with Dog for a long time to come.

"Let's try it," continued Hawkins. "I...I can't stand it in here much longer."

We both moved at the same time and nearly got ourselves wedged tightly in the middle of the culvert. I guess it made us both pretty nervous.

"We have to go one at a time," I said to Hawkins.

"Who's first?" he asked me and his voice was getting hoarse.

I wanted to go first and then I thought of Dog. "You can go first," I said generously and Hawkins didn't seem to realize that he'd been set up. He moved forward eagerly and cautiously exited the culvert.

I waited to see what was going to happen. There was no angry barking and no squealing from Hawkins so I decided that it must be safe. I pushed my way out of the culvert and looked around.

To my surprise it was already dark. The stars twinkled overhead and the moon sent shadows dancing across the grasses at our feet.

"Where are we?" I asked Hawkins.

"I have no idea," he answered.

"Mother will be worried," I said and my shivering started again. I was worried too.

"Well, I'm hungry," said Hawkins. I wasn't surpised. He was always hungry.

"We need to find Mother," I told him and my voice was trembling. I knew that if we could find her all of our troubles would be over.

I turned toward the lane. I was sure that it was the way we had come.

"Wait," demanded Hawkins, "you can't go that way."

"It's the way we came," I insisted.

"Yes, and it's the way Dog came too. If we go that way, we'll run smack into him again."

That stopped me in my tracks. Hawkins sneezed again and I quickly looked up the lane, hoping that his noisy explosions wouldn't bring Dog back on the run.

All seemed quiet and I began to breathe normally again.

"What are we going to do?" I asked Hawkins.

"Well, we'll just have to try to find our own way - around the farmyard," he said matter-of-factly. I had to admire his reasoning.

I nodded my head in agreement. Then fear gripped me again.

"How far around?" I asked him.

"I dunno," he responded with a shrug of his shoulders and another sneeze. "Far enough that Dog won't see us."

I shivered again.

"How long will that take?" I asked and my voice was trembling.

"I dunno," said Hawkins again.

I stood and shivered some more. Afraid to move, yet reluctant to stay.

"This is all your fault," I hurled at Hawkins but he wouldn't accept the blame.

"Get real," he snuffled, "you were just as anxious to crawl out under that gate as I was."

I had to admit the truth of the statement - at least inwardly. I said nothing to Hawkins.

"So, what are we going to do?" I asked at last.

"Well, we won't get anywhere standing here," he responded. He started to walk away from me in the opposite direction than I knew the farmyard to be.

"Wait," I squealed. I didn't agree with where he was going, but I sure didn't want to be left alone.

We trudged on and on. I was sure that Hawkins was totally lost.

"I don't think that we are even on our farm any more," I muttered.

"Maybe not," said Hawkins. "But we have to go the long way around to get back to our yard."

"Does it have to be *this* long a way around?" I mumbled. My back was aching, my feet were tired and my stomach was totally empty.

Hawkins cut to his left again and we started off at a slow trot. We were much too tired now to travel any faster.

"Mother will be worried," I said again.

The moon was changing position in the sky and I knew that the night was far spent.

Through fields and over ditches, across grassy pastures and around ponds, under fences and between bushes, we plodded wearily on.

Then the most wonderful thing happened. We crawled under another fence and there, right before our eyes, was a magnificent garden. For one moment I thought that we had completed our circle and arrived at the garden on our own farm. But I noticed by the moonlight that this garden was planned differently than the garden we had admired through the wires of our barnyard fence. The plants were all arranged in little beds rather than in long, straight rows.

It didn't matter to us. Here was a garden and we

were starving. Without another word we both went right to work helping ourselves generously.

By the time the moon tucked sleepily into bed and the sun pushed its way vigorously into the sky, we were both so full our sides bulged.

"Where do you think home is?" I asked Hawkins around a mouthful of juicy carrots.

"I dunno," he responded and then yawned.

"Do you think we should go find it?" I asked.

"Yeah," he agreed. "I guess we should, but not right now. I'm much too tired to walk another step."

I looked at him. He really was much too full to walk another step, I thought as I studied him.

I was too tired, and too full, to argue.

"Maybe we should take a nap first," I suggested.

"Let's," he agreed

We pushed our way in among the turnip plants so that the sun wouldn't beat down on us too brightly and snuggled up together. It felt wonderful to curl up, full and without the threat of Dog. I was sure that when we had taken a little nap we would be able to find our way home again with no problem. That was before I was aware that we had trespassed and were camping out in a neighbor's garden.

CHAPTER TEN

HOME AGAIN

A noise nearby awoke me. I could hear a soft thud, thud, thud, as though someone was beating at the earth. I hated to stir. My tummy was still full and I was warm and cuddled up with Hawkins. I knew if I moved I would wake him up. From past experience I knew that Hawkins didn't take too kindly to being awakened from a good nap.

I lay still and listened. Thud. Thud. Thud. The noise kept on and it seemed to be getting closer. I eased myself as carefully as I could away from Hawkins. He grumbled in his sleep but he didn't open his eyes.

I made my way between the big turnip leaves and poked my head out to see what was going on. I hoped that the farm dog hadn't found us.

It wasn't Dog that made the sound. Woman was there and she had a stick in her hand with a thing on the end of it and she kept beating at the ground, thud, thud, thud. Wherever she hit, the earth was lifted up. It looked much easier for earth-turning than rooting.

I was not afraid of Woman. All of the family that lived at our farm were kind and gentle. Best of all, they always brought us food. Delicious things to eat. I wasn't sure if I knew this Woman because her back was turned to me as she thudded her stick at the ground. I didn't think it would be hard to get her attention.

Without even a squeal of introduction I hastened over to her and pressed my cold, wet snout against her warm, bare ankle.

You have never heard such a noise. It frightened me so badly that I raced back to the turnip patch again, squealing out my fear as I ran. The commotion woke Hawkins and he dashed out of the turnips, tail in the air and voice screaming that we were being attacked. "Mother! Mother!" he screamed. "Save us! Save us! A monster is after us!"

I knew that it wasn't a monster. It was just Woman. I couldn't figure out why she just stayed there and danced and screamed.

A strange man came running, his eyes wild with concern.

"What is it? What is it?" I heard him call as he ran.

The Woman still screamed. He reached her and shook her slightly by the arms. "What is it?"

"Pigs," she shrieked, pointing a finger in the direction that Hawkins had disappeared.

I stood shivering in my tracks, tangled among some cords that had supported a group of large plants. I knew if the one with that stick in her hand came my way I would need to make a dash for it. I began to gather myself together for one big plunge that would free me.

"Pigs?" said the man. "Where?"

Woman looked around until she spotted me entrapped by the cords. "There," she yelled. "Right there."

When she got a good look at me, she stopped screaming.

"That little fella?" asked the man in disbelief.

"He startled me," she hastened to explain. "Came right up and stuck his snout on my leg. I had no idea what it was."

They began to laugh together.

"Well, little or not," the man said at last, "he doesn't belong here."

"Probably belongs to the Browns. There are at least two of them. I'm sure I saw one run that way."

The man made a move toward me but I was all ready for him. I wasn't sure what he intended to do with me and I wasn't too anxious to find out. With one mighty lunge I sprang forward and raced across the garden, dragging rope, stakes and plants right along with me. As I ran I gathered more plants, uprooting them from their growing spots. I am sure that I made quite a spectacle and I know that I left quite a trail.

"Stop him," cried Woman. "He's going to ruin my whole garden."

My flight brought Hawkins out from his hiding place. With a wild scream of protest he began to run along with me. Around and around we went with Man close at our heels and Woman right after him, still waving her stick in the air.

Then their farm dog decided to get in on the act. That was what really brought fear to my heart. I didn't care to be nipped again and I guess Hawkins felt that way too. We ran and ran until we were panting and puffing and tearing up more and more stakes and more and more plants. Finally Man and his dog cornered us against a wire enclosure. There was no place left to run.

Without a word the man lunged for us, catching Hawkins with one big hand and me with the other. I was sure that he'd turn us over to Dog but he didn't. I felt his hand on my hind legs and then I felt myself being swung in a big arc, my head down and my hind legs stretched out by his hold.

Back and forth, back and forth, I swung. Below me the ground kept tipping this way, then that. I was feeling sick to my stomach. Gradually the arcs diminished in size and I was being carried away. Out of the corner of my eye I could see Hawkins. He, too, was wrong-side up and hanging helplessly, head down. I heard him protest. He didn't like the position any better than I did.

Soon Man reached wherever it was he was taking us. He called back to Woman, "Call the Browns. Tell them we have a couple of their piglets here."

Woman laid aside her stick and went into the place where they lived.

Man put us in a little wire pen and set us back on our feet again. Mine felt too weak to support me. I slumped right down on my tummy and stayed there. For a moment I lay there trying hard to make the world stop moving about me. At last I dared to open

my eyes. We really had stopped swinging from side to side. Relieved, I pushed up on my feet and nosed my way around the little pen. Hawkins was just opening his eyes.

As soon as he saw me he jumped up and joined me. We were anxious to find our way out of the small enclosure so that we could find Mother and the farm where we lived. I had really had enough of the outside world for the present.

But there was no way out. We looked and looked and thrust our snouts in here and there but the wire enclosure held fast.

We heard a noise and a big farm truck pulled into the yard. And there was our Man. He climbed from the truck on one side and Girl jumped out of the other side. Man went to the porch to talk to the strange Man and Woman, but Girl ran directly to the pen where we were enclosed.

"There you are," she said, stretching her hand into the pen. "I was worried about you."

I tried to tell her that we were pretty worried, too, but she went right on talking.

"How did you ever find your way over here?"

I told her that we hadn't found our way anywhere. We had just sort of ended up in the garden.

"Well, you are safe and sound now. We'll take you home."

That sounded great to me. I let her stroke my back and rub my ears.

Man talked to the other Man and Woman for a long time. They even went out to the garden. I don't know what they talked about. Maybe the turnips.

At last Man was back. He lifted us out of the pen one at a time but he didn't swing us head down. He held our middles and pulled us up close against his chest, then placed us carefully in a little box in the back of the truck.

It didn't take long to get back to our own yard but I didn't care much for the trip. The truck rumbled and bumped and swayed back and forth. Now I was afraid that I was really going to be sick.

At last we bumped to a stop. Girl came running to get me, while Man lifted out Hawkins. They carried us toward the barn and back through the gate. I could see Mother and our sisters and brother snuggled together on the straw bed. They were having a morning feeding. I could hardly wait to join them.

With one last scratch behind the ears, Girl lowered me to the ground. I ran off toward Mother as fast as I could. I could hear Hawkins right behind me.

"Mother! Mother!" we squealed. "We're back! We're back!"

With a mighty lunge Mother was on her feet, scattering the piglets all over the straw. She wheeled to greet us, grunting and squealing her pleasure.

We greeted her first, pushing our snouts against her and telling her how glad we were to see her. Then, one by one, we greeted the rest of the family.

"Where'd you go?" asked Higgins. "How'd you get out? Did you see anything? Tell me about it."

Hawkins and I just looked at one another. We

had plenty to talk about, but I guess neither one of us was quite ready to talk yet.

I know that I just wanted to curl up in the straw beside Mother and feel safe and protected and cared for. I guess Hawkins felt the same way for he turned to Higgins and said, "Later, little Bro. Later."

The next several days were quiet. Hawkins and I had enjoyed enough adventure for some time. We were content to stay close to Mother, to play in the Hole and to snatch snacks from the feeding trough of the older pigs when we could get close enough to pilfer.

Higgins wanted to learn all about our adventure. Though I figured that it was exciting enough as it was, I guess Hawkins didn't. He kept adding little things as he told the story to sort of 'liven it up,' he said. It had sure seemed lively enough to me just as it was.

We had been home for about a week when another storm blew in. Mother eyed the sky with a worried look on her face and then called to all of us to join her in the shed.

We didn't protest. We didn't care much for the cold rain on our backs.

The wind and noise came first. The clouds seemed to boil over our heads and lightning danced across the sky. Thunder crashed, then rumbled away.

It would have been fascinating had it not been so scary.

I cuddled as close to Mother as I could get and closed my eyes tightly to try to miss the lightning. I never could. The brightness penetrated my eyelids. Then I listened as the angry thunder slammed across the sky.

Rain began to splatter against the tin roof overhead. It was so loud that it almost drowned out the thunder. Almost. A flash of bright lightning lit up the shed. I didn't even have time to close my eyes. Then a loud crash came smashing right into our world. I was sure that I felt the barn tremble. We all squealed. Even Mother let out a little grunt of fright.

Mother had just calmed us down a bit when the door flew open and Man was there. He didn't come as he usually did, with slow steps and soft voice and a pail of tempting food in his hand.

He was running and his voice was loud and excited. He carried no pail and Dog was close at his heels.

At that very instant I smelled something that I had never smelled before. It wasn't good and I knew that it wasn't something to eat.

"Rex," Man shouted to Dog, "get them all out of here."

Dog began to bark. It echoed in the rafters of the shed and bounced off one wall, then the other. To me it sounded like a dozen angry, excited dogs barking. I didn't know which way to run.

Mother knew. She lunged up and called as she headed for the small door that took us out into the farmyard.

"Come! Come quickly! Now!"

As soon as we could get our feet under us, we followed.

I knew that we were running out into the cold
rain and I couldn't figure out why. I hated the rain
on my back. I hated the crashes of thunder and the
bright zig-zagging of blinding light. It seemed
unfair of Man and Dog to come running in, yelling
and barking and flailing arms to scare us out into the
gathering   night.

When we arrived outside, the whole yard was in
turmoil. Mrs. Red Sow was there, anxiously calling to her eight young who were now too big to
stay with their mother anymore. Yet, she gathered
them around her, counting and recounting them.

Mrs. Young Sow was there, her small piglets
cowering around her legs, crying and shivering,
half-scared to death. She tried hard to console them,
but she looked as frightened as they did.

Mother called us all to her and made sure that
each one of us had left the barn-shed. It still didn't
make any sense to me, but I answered when Mother
called my name, pressing against her to find some
warmth and reassurance.

Horse family was there. They snorted and flung
their heads, raced to the end of the yard, tossed
their manes and ran back again, wheeling and plung-
ing and nearly running over anything that got in
their way. I had never seen them act so strangely
before.

Cow family was there. They huddled together
at the far side of the yard, calling and bawling and
checking on their calves. The calves didn't romp
now but pressed close against their mothers.

Man was still there. He raced here and there

shouting to Woman and Girl. I couldn't hear his words and couldn't understand his actions.

Dog was still there too. He raced around even faster than Man. Now and then he let out a yip but he had stopped his excited, continuous barking.

I huddled up against Mother.

"Let's go back in," I wailed. "I don't like it out here."

Mother said nothing.

"Isn't it sad?" spoke Mrs. Red Sow. "I have never seen the like in my life."

"What will we ever do now?" whimpered Mrs. Young Sow. "My babies are much too young to be out in this terrible weather."

"Don't worry, Dear," said Mother gently, "Man will think of something."

They were all looking toward our home as they spoke. I was pushing against Mother with my back toward the barn, and I had no idea what they were speaking of.

I wheeled around to look and there was our barn, shed and all, with bright flames shooting up into the blackness of the night sky. Billowing black poured up to meet the dark clouds that hung above it. I knew now what the strange, awful smell was.

"Stop it! Stop it!" I urged Mother

"No one can stop it," she said sadly. "Not even Man."

"What is it?" cried Bee-Bee.

"It's fire."

"Where did it come from?" demanded Othelia.

"The storm. The lightning brought it," answered Mrs. Red Sow.

"I don't like it," I insisted. "I wish it would go away."

"No one likes it," sighed Mother. "But at least we are out with our chops, thanks to Man and Dog."

I had been a little angry with Man and Dog for making all the fuss. Now I realized that they were saving our lives.

"What will we ever do now?" said Mrs. Young Sow again. "My poor, poor babies."

Mother turned then. I guess she knew that someone had to do something.

"The straw pile is a safe distance away," she said to Mrs. Red Sow. "We'll nose down to find dry bedding and we'll all sleep there tonight."

Mother led the way to the straw pile and the other two mothers and their young followed. We were all cold and scared and nervous about our future. I guess we just snuggled in the straw together. There was no pushing or shoving or fighting that night. We all had other things on our minds.

CHAPTER ELEVEN
NEW QUARTERS

The next day the farm was a hive of activity. Man was there, moving this way and that, toting this and that, swinging one thing, then another, building, pounding, calling, hurrying. From morning to night, it seemed that he never stopped.

Other men were with him and they worked together. Where the barn had stood, there was nothing now. Nothing but emptiness and black seeping smoke that bothered my eyes and my throat. Man and his helpers worked in the shadow of the smoke and put a fence across the corner of our yard. Our big, free-moving space was now more confined. We still had our straw pile. We still had the Hole and we still had our feeding troughs but we didn't have as much room anymore.

Then, to add to the space problem, small pens were moved in along one fence and a shed was moved against another.

I was all ready to move toward the big shed but Mother stopped me.

"That will be for Cow family," she told me.

"But I like that big one," I insisted.

"This will be our home for now," said Mother,

"one of these smaller ones."

It hardly looked like there would be room for our whole family in such a small space. Mother led the way in and we reluctantly followed. It sure wasn't as nice as the shed we had lived in. Othelia said so.

"It will be fine," said Mother. "It will keep the rain off our backs and provide shade from the hot sun. That is all we need."

I wasn't too happy with the arrangement but I shrugged my shoulders and decided to make the best of it.

Mrs Red Sow chose another of the small houses. Some of her young joined her but they couldn't all fit so the rest moved into another. Mrs. Young Sow looked very relieved to get her small piglets into a place of their own.

Girl came to check on us. She seemed particularly interested in Hawkins and me.

"You're okay," she said as she ran her hand over my back. "I was scared I'd lose you for my project. Or you." She turned and reached out a hand to Hawkins.

I could see the glint in his eye and I knew that he was still determined to be the one chosen by Girl. I didn't say anything but I set my jaw. I was just as determined.

It took several days for the barn to stop smouldering. Finally Man came in with a big, noisy machine and pushed the rest of the burning piles aside. Soon the spot became even busier than before. When I asked Mother about all of the commotion, she smiled happily and informed us that Man was building us a new barn.

We were all excited about that. But, oh my, it seemed to take an awfully long time - and Man had lots of help with the work, too.

After watching them for a few days, we got tired of the project and went on with other things. We still felt that our house and yard was too small for all of us to inhabit together, but there wasn't much that we could do about it. The older pigs spent most of their time in the Hole. And true to what our elders had said, there were things growing after the rains had come. Mother and the others loved to root out the shoots and roots and smacked loudly as they savored the small delicacies.

We rooted, too. I never seemed to find much that was worth eating. I just rooted because there wasn't much else to do.

Hawkins always pretended that he found all sorts of good things. He'd smack and "umm" and shake his head with deep satisfaction, his eyes closed and a silly grin on his face.

I always wondered if he really had found something or if he was just trying to make the rest of us jealous.

One day as he chomped and slurped, he let out a sudden yell. I was close enough to see exactly what happened but Mother wasn't. She came running, grunting out her concern as she ran. I'm sure that she thought something dreadful had happened to Hawkins. She seemed relieved to see him still on his feet.

"What happened? Are you all right?" she asked him, nosing him with her snout to make sure that he was still in one piece.

Hawkins couldn't even answer. He was still shaking his head as though something hurt. I could see that tears had sprung into his eyes so I knew he wasn't bluffing this time. Hawkins would do anything to keep from showing tears.

"Are you all right?" Mother repeated anxiously. "What happened?"

Hawkins slowly let his mouthful of rooted goodies trickle to the ground. He was still wincing. He shook his head slowly. When his mouth was totally empty, he shook his head again. Finally he spoke to Mother, "I chomped down on a sharp stone," he said sheepishly.

He was red-faced now. Mother had taught us to roll things around in our mouths, sorting out the good from the bad with our tongues. In Hawkins' haste to impress us with all of the good things that he was finding, he had forgotten that lesson.

I was sure that Mother would remind him again. Though I hated to miss seeing it, I knew that I was about to snicker. I moved away hurriedly so that I could laugh without being caught.

That afternoon I stretched out in the mud along with my family members and shut my eyes against the hot summer sun. We were too big to do much playing anymore. Besides it was much nicer to just lie there and enjoy the mud. I had seen the family of Mrs. Young Sow eyeing the Hole. One day soon they would be diving in, making mud fly out in all directions. I wasn't crazy about having my relaxation interrupted by small flying bodies.

Anyway, my thoughts were not really on the younger piglets. They were on food. Now that I was bigger and the scare had gone out of me, I kept thinking about that garden that Hawkins and I had raided. I guess he must have been thinking about it too. One day as I lazed in the mud I felt something poke me. When I opened my eyes I found that it was Hawkins.

I was about to grunt angrily at him when I noticed the shine in his eyes. I started to open my mouth to ask what he was up to, but he nodded his head toward the inner yard. Slowly I got up and followed him out of the Hole.

"What's this about?" I asked as soon as we were out of earshot.

Hawkins just looked at me with that sparkle still in his eyes.

"You know that temporary fence," he said, with a nod toward it. "Well, it's not as pig-tight as the old one."

"What do you mean?" I asked in a whisper.

"There are places we can squeeze through," he informed me.

My eyes widened. "Have you tried it?" I asked.

"Not yet. I was waiting for you. We can go together."

"Oh, no," I said and turned my back on Hawkins. "Remember the last time?"

"Hey, we got back safe and sound, didn't we?" he reminded me and nudged me around to face him again.

"Sure," I said, "after being nipped by Dog, nearly frozen to death in the cold water of a culvert, lost for the night, so tired of running that my legs felt like they would fall off, and then screamed at and chased by a crazy Woman with a stick in her hand."

"Aw, c'mon," said Hawkins. "It wasn't all that bad. Remember the garden?"

I remembered the garden. I had been having dreams about it ever since I got over the worst of my fright.

"We don't even know where to find the garden," I reminded Hawkins.

"Well, we don't have to find it. There is a garden just the other side of that fence."

Hawkins nodded his head in the direction of our farm garden.

"How about Dog?" I asked.

"What about Dog?"

"He'll catch us," I said and my voice rose as I spoke.

"Sh-h-h," cautioned Hawkins. He cast a glance toward the Hole where the others all slumbered in the sun.

"It's a crazy idea," I said to Hawkins. "You know that Dog doesn't miss a thing that goes on around here."

"Then we won't go to the garden."

"So why bother getting out?" I asked.

"We'll head for the orchard. That's further away. Dog won't notice us there."

"The orchard?"

"Yeah. I've heard Geese talking about it. They say there are little apples all over the ground."

"You mean - like Man sometimes brings to us?" I loved those little apples. They were one of my favorite snacks.

"Right!" said Hawkins. "Just like that. And they are all over in the orchard grass. I heard Geese say so."

I wondered since when Hawkins had been on speaking terms with Geese, but I held my tongue.

I was still doubtful about Hawkins' plan but the thought of the orchard apples did intrigue me. I cast a glance over my shoulder to make sure that Mother was still sleeping and then nodded my head at Hawkins.

"Let's see your hole in the fence," I said to him.

Hawkins moved forward slowly. He kept peering this way and that to make sure no one would spoil his plan. At last we reached the fence and he led me to a spot in the make-shift arrangement. There was a hole there all right, but when Hawkins pushed his nose into it, he realized that it wasn't big enough to let him pass. I was about to say, "I told you so," but Hawkins didn't wait for that. He moved on to another spot and pushed and shoved at it. It wasn't big enough either.

"Just wait," Hawkins said in answer to my impatient shrug. "There are lots of other places."

He moved on to another one of them. Sure enough, after shoving and rooting and pushing this way and that, Hawkins began to enlarge the hole. It wasn't long until he was down on his knees pushing and wriggling his way through the opening. I knew if he could make it, I could. He was still just a little bigger than me.

As soon as we had escaped the yard, we began to look for Dog. I finally spotted his tail sticking out from between the rails of the porch.

"He's sleeping," I said to Hawkins in a whisper. "Over there at the house."

That was a piece of good luck.

"Where's the orchard?" I asked Hawkins.

"I think that way," he answered me.

"What do you mean, you think?" I retorted angrily. "Don't you know?"

"That's the way Geese always go," he replied. It still didn't sound too exact to me.

Hawkins moved off to our right.

"Where are you going?" I asked him.

"We have to go around the fowl yard," he replied.

"Why?" I demanded, thinking of the feeding troughs and the delicious food they always held.

"Because they make too much noise," argued Hawkins. "They'll call Dog."

Now that made sense. I knew what kind of clamor the farmyard fowl could make. They would call Dog for sure. I followed Hawkins.

I'm not sure how, but Hawkins did manage to get us to the orchard. It was a long, round-about trek but it sure was worth it. There were apples there. Oh, not apples all over the ground like Hawkins had promised, but scattered here and there. A good snout could search them out.

By foraging about, we filled our tummies. The apples were small and they were green, but they were delicious.

"I think we'd better get home," said Hawkins around the apples in his mouth. "Mother will soon miss us."

"We'll come back again tomorrow," I mumbled as I chomped, and Hawkins agreed.

We both felt very pleased with ourselves. We had made a great discovery. We headed back the same way that we had come. I looked for Dog's tail on the porch but didn't see it. I did hope that he had found another place to nap.

We had almost reached our hole in the fence when I spotted Dog. He was coming toward us on the run. He hadn't taken very many steps before he opened his mouth and began his loud barking. It scared us almost out of our skins.

We both ran for our fence. Hawkins got there just a bit ahead of me and he made a dash for the opening. I was right at his heels, ready to duck through before Dog reached us.

I don't really know what happened. Maybe in his hurry Hawkins had chosen the wrong hole. Or maybe he didn't hit it at quite the right angle. Or maybe he had just eaten so many apples that he was too full to get through. For whatever reason, he got stuck. And there I was with Dog fast approaching and no place to hide.

I tell you, no one could have slept through what happened next. Hawkins was squealing, Dog was yapping, I was running back and forth along the fence screaming for Mother to rescue me before Dog tore me to bits. From the Mud Hole came all of the pig family, screaming and grunting and shouting for us to get ourselves out of that fence and back to safety.

What a racket!

All of the noise set off the fowl in the next yard and they began to cackle and honk and quack and gobble. The din was almost more than ears could bear.

Man soon appeared, running toward the commotion. Woman came after him, her broom still in her hand.

"Get some pliers," I heard Man call to Girl who came running along behind the procession. Girl ran quickly to a small shed by the fowl pens.

Man fell on his knees beside Hawkins and tried to hold his squirming body so that the wires of the fence would cause no further damage. I could see that Hawkins had already scratched his back in more than one place.

Girl handed the pliers to Man and I closed my eyes. I was sure that he was going to do something dreadful to my errant brother. I heard a few snips and then a scrambling and I looked up in time to see Hawkins go scurrying into our yard, still screaming at the top of his lungs. Mother was there to meet him and he ran directly to her.

It seemed that they had all forgotten about me. I stood shivering and shaking hoping that they wouldn't notice me in the corner, but I wasn't to be so lucky. Dog, of course, couldn't keep his loud mouth closed. He soon drew everyone's attention to the fact that I was also where I shouldn't be.

"Open the gate," Man called to Girl and she did.

If they would just have stood aside, I would have ducked in quickly but they insisted on gathering around me, waving arms and the broom and shouting and barking until it scared me out of my wits. In my confusion, I almost broke through the line and ran in the wrong direction.

Luckily, I noticed my error in time to duck back around and head for the gate and safety. As I scrambled to the far end of our yard, I wasn't sure that I wanted to listen to any more of Hawkins' schemes. My legs were trembling with fright and my full tummy no longer felt comfortable. In fact, I had the feeling that I might be sick. All that I wanted to do was to find Mother and rest for a long, long time.

CHAPTER TWELVE
PENNED

I was sure that Hawkins would be cured of his wandering after our adventure. I wasn't anxious to try getting out again. But I guess Hawkins looked at things differently. The scratches on his back and sides had barely healed when he was at me again.

"Want to go back to the orchard?"

I looked at him like he had lost his senses.

"I know where we can get out," he continued.

"You must be mad," I said quite frankly. "Don't you remember what happened the last time?"

Hawkins glanced over his shoulder at the largest scratch on his right side.

"'Course I remember," he answered sharply, "but it's healed, hasn't it? It wasn't really that bad."

"Well, you sure hollered like it was bad enough," I reminded him.

"I seem to recall you doing a bit of hollering yourself," he retorted. I reddened a bit. The fact was, I didn't have any scratches or nips, yet I had been just as noisy and just as scared.

I wasn't sure what to say next so I didn't say anything.

"Want to go?" Hawkins prompted.

"I saw Man fix that hole in the fence," I informed Hawkins.

"Ah-h. All he did was string a tiny little piece of wire across it. I could push that aside easily."

I hadn't been back to check on the fence but I was sure that Hawkins had examined it.

"You sure?"

"Sure, I'm sure. All it is - one little skinny wire. Saw it myself."

"Aw, I dunno," I hesitated. "We always get ourselves in a heap of trouble."

"The wind blew pretty hard last night," said Hawkins. I wondered what that had to do with it. I guess he knew I'd be wondering for he hurried to explain.

"That's what brings the apples down. Goose said so. It's the wind. It shakes the trees and the apples fall to the ground. There should be lots and lots of apples on the ground now."

The very thought of the apples caused me to smack my lips. Still, I was hesitant. Mother had been quite angry with us the last time we had gotten ourselves in trouble.

"Mother doesn't like us to..."

"She doesn't need to know. We'll slip out under that little wire and eat our fill and slip back in with no one the wiser."

"It never seems to work the way you plan it," I reminded Hawkins.

"Well, are you going or aren't you?" he pressured me.

I shook my head slowly. It was so tempting, but I knew that Mother would really be cross with us.

"I don't think so," I said at last. The words seemed awfully hard to get out.

"Sissy," hissed Hawkins.

"You going?" I asked, hoping that Hawkins would change his mind if he had to go alone.

"Sure I'm going. Maybe I'll let Higgins go with me. He isn't chicken."

I hated to be called chicken but I had made up my mind.

"You'd better leave Higgins here," I told Hawkins. "If you get him in trouble, Mother will really be cross with you."

I guess Hawkins took my word for it. He cast one glance toward the Hole at the end of the yard, then pushed his way past me and headed for the fence.

I followed. I had made up my mind that I wasn't going with Hawkins. But I couldn't resist seeing the skinny little wire that he said was between him and an orchard full of fallen apples.

I expected Hawkins to be exaggerating again but, when we reached the fence, I was surprised to see that he was right. All that stretched across the hole we had made when we forced our way through the fence, was one thin little wire.

"See," said Hawkins triumphantly, "I told you so."

I could hardly believe that Man would think that would hold in hungry pigs. Maybe he had posted Dog on the other side of the fence.

I peered through the openings and looked around.

Dog was nowhere in sight. The way looked clear.

"You sure you don't want to go?" Hawkins asked me again. I just stood firm and shook my head.

"You can go first if you like," offered Hawkins.

"I'm not going," I repeated, irritation edging my voice.

"Okay," shrugged Hawkins. "Have it your way, but you can't say that you weren't invited."

Oh, I wanted to go. I could just taste those green apples. It would be so easy. So easy. Nothing but that little piece of wire separating us from freedom and the apple orchard.

I squeezed my eyes shut and braced my feet. "No," I stated firmly, "I'm not going."

Hawkins shrugged again. I knew that I'd had my last invitation.

Hawkins moved to the fence and reached out with his wet snout to push aside that one little wire. I watched. The moment he touched it, his whole body jerked and he threw his head in the air and screamed as though he had been stabbed with a skewer.

The backward jerk had put him on his knees. He just stayed there, shaking his head and squealing in frustration or pain, I wasn't sure which. I had no idea what had happened.

Mother came running. She must have thought that I had done something to Hawkins for she called out as she passed me, "What have you done?"

"Nothing," I yelled back. "Honest! Nothing."

Mother nosed Hawkins to his feet and checked him over to try to find the source of his great pain.

There were no marks on his body. At least none that I could see.

"What is it?" cried Mother. "What happened?"

Still Hawkins said nothing. Tears had gathered in his eyes and he kept shaking his head.

"What happened?" Mother turned to me to ask the question.

"I'm...I'm not sure," I stammered.

"What did he do?"

"Nothing. I mean he just...just reached out his snout to...to..." How could I say that Hawkins' plans for pushing through the hole again had been interrupted?

"He touched his nose...on that fence?" asked Mother, her eyes wide.

"Not the...not the whole fence," I stuttered, "just...just that one little..."

"Oh, my!" said Mother. "Oh, my!"

Mrs. Red Sow came puffing up. "What happened?" she demanded.

"He touched his nose on the electric fence," explained Mother.

"Oh, my!" said Mrs. Red Sow. "Oh, my!"

I still hadn't figured out the problem.

"What electric fence?" I asked Mother.

"That one," she said pointing her snout toward the one little wire. Quickly she jerked it back as though she feared something might jump out at her.

"What does it do?" I asked next.

"It stings. It bites. Oh, my, how it smarts," she said in explanation.

"Have you...have you...tested it?" I asked.

"Once. When I was very young." Mother shook her head. "I'll tell you one thing," she said with emphasis, "no pig ever tries it twice."

Mrs. Red Sow shook her head and worked her mammoth jaws. "No pig," she echoed. "No pig ever tries it twice."

"Come," said Mother to Hawkins. "Come to the Hole. The cool mud might take some of the soreness out of it."

Mother led the way and Hawkins followed silently. I don't know if the cool mud helped but I noticed that he didn't do any rooting for the next few days.

At last the new barn stood tall and shining in our yard. The makeshift fence was removed and the temporary shelters were taken away. We had our big yard back again. All of us were glad about that.

"I can hardly wait to see the new milking parlor," I heard one of the Cow family say to another.

"I do hope there is more room," said the second one. "I used to have to bump my side right up against Rosie whenever they milked me."

"I know," said the first, "it was so tight..."

I moved away so I didn't hear the last of the conversation. I was much more interested in the pen that my family would be moving into.

It didn't happen quite the way I expected. We were shown a new door and Dog helped to direct us through it. When we got inside, Mother was placed in one pen and my sisters, brothers and myself in another. It seemed very strange to be separated from Mother but she spoke to us through the boards and told us not to worry. There always came a time when youngsters needed to be on their own and we would be well fed, she assured us. Man would see to that.

I was just starting to get used to being without Mother when there was another surprise for me. Man and Girl came to the pens. Man leaned on the top board while Girl climbed in with us.

"Is it time?" she asked and Man nodded.

"Have you decided?" asked Man. This time it was Girl's turn to nod.

"Him," she said. She pointed a finger at me.

"The other one's still bigger," Man went on.

I held my breath. I was afraid that she would change her mind and I did so much want to be the one chosen.

"I know, but I have always liked this one. And besides, the bigger one has the scars from the scratches on his back and side," said the girl.

"Yes, you're right," said Man. "The scratches do make a difference."

I was very thankful that I hadn't gotten myself tangled up in that fence.

Before I knew what was happening, I was being herded through another small door and into an adjoining pen. I expected the rest of the family to follow me but the door was shut firmly behind me. I was all alone.

I could still see them. I could still talk to them. But I could no longer curl up with them at nap time or join in their squabbles at the feeding trough. In fact, I had my own clean, warm bed and my very own feeding trough. I had the whole breakfast or dinner or supper all to myself. At first it was hard to get used to. I was surprised at how much I missed my family. Even Hawkins. Still, I must admit that I felt special. I knew that I was being treated better than the others.

I was given food that I had never tasted before. I loved it. And I was given fresh, clean bedding every day and was even washed and brushed and petted and pampered. I loved the company of Girl almost as much as I had loved the company of my family.

From next door my family watched all of the strange happenings in my pen.

"Why all the fussing?" asked Hawkins. "What did you do to deserve all of the special attention?"

I was tempted to boast a bit. I wanted to say, "She thinks I'm cute. Remember? She likes me best," but I didn't try to answer his question. The fact was, I really had no idea why I was getting special treatment except that she kept referring to her project. But I loved it.

"What is it they put in your trough?" asked Millie, or Tillie. I still couldn't tell them apart.

"It's...it's food. Good food. But it's different," I tried to explain.

I'd sure like to try it," grunted Hawkins.

"You'd like it," I assured him. That didn't seem to make Hawkins feel any better.

The next strange thing that happened surprised me even more. Girl came with a bit of odd leather and fastened it around one of my legs. To this she clipped a leather strap and we began to take walks together. It was wonderful to get out into the bright sun and the fresh air. I hoped that she would lead me to the Hole sometime but she never did.

We walked and paused, turned this way and that way, walked and paused. Sometimes she scolded me. Sometimes she praised me and slipped me a piece of green apple. I soon discovered what it was that she wanted me to do before she offered me another treat. I liked the outings, but I liked the apples even more.

"He's doing great, isn't he, Dad?" she said one day. Man was leaning on a pitchfork handle watching our walking and pausing.

"He is," Man agreed. "And he is filling out nicely, too."

"I'll bet he's the biggest one in the litter now," Girl continued.

I thought she must have forgotten about Hawkins. He had always been bigger than me.

"Do you think we have a chance, Dad?" Girl questioned.

Man smiled. "He's a nice-looking pig. And you've done a good job with him. Sure, I think you have a good chance."

Girl looked pleased about that.

"C'mon," she said to me. "Let's practice a little bit more."

Dog trotted up beside us. I wasn't afraid of him anymore. He never nipped me and he seldom barked. He just whined softly to Girl.

"What do you think, Rex?" asked Girl. "Do you think we have a chance at the fair?"

Rex didn't answer her question. He just licked her hand with a long, wet tongue. But I felt my head swelling. I was beginning to think that I was one pretty special pig.

CHAPTER THIRTEEN

THE FAIR

I heard much about the Fair over the next few weeks but I had no idea what folks were talking about. I did gather that it was important to Girl - and also to her two young brothers who were always questioning her about it.

"How much longer 'til the Fair, Jill?"

"Will he be ready in time?"

"Do you think he knows how to walk right?"

"Is he fat enough?"

"Well, is it the right kind of fat?"

"Will you win?"

They were always asking questions as they tagged along behind us on our daily walks about the farm. She answered some of their questions. At other times she just laughed and said, "We'll just have to wait and see."

I had no idea if Fair was something to eat, some place to go, or something to sleep on. Girl never explained. One day I found myself getting a very special bath and a special brushing. I knew that something was different about this day.

Girl put me in a special pen and I laid down on the fresh straw and waited. It wasn't long before she

appeared again. It looked like she'd had a special
bath and a special brushing as well.

All the family soon gathered in the yard. My pen
was lifted into the back of the truck. Man climbed
in one door and Girl in the other and we were off.
Through the mesh across one end of my pen I could
see Woman and Boys climbing into another truck
and they followed us. I had no idea where we were
all going.

After a long time of bumping and swaying, we
arrived at a big field. It contained many, many build-
ings and pens, some small and some big. Also many,
many milling people and families were gathered
there.

Girl bounded from the truck and came back to
check on me.

"Well, what do you think of the Fair?" she
asked in an excited voice.

"So this is Fair," I thought to myself, a bit disappointed. I had expected something - something
more special. Something more fitting for a special
pig like me.

Around me there seemed to be total confusion.
Things moved this way and that way and back again.
I wasn't sure what I thought of Fair.

The day was warm. I was glad that Man and Girl
placed my pen on the ground in the shade. Soon I
grew tired of watching all of the commotion and
stretched out on the soft straw for a sleep.

It was afternoon before Girl came back for me.

"It's our turn. It's our turn," she said excitedly.
She opened the gate of my small pen and slipped the

leash onto the strap around my ankle.

"Come now," she coaxed. "Be good. You must be on your best behavior."

We walked around together, moving, then pausing, turning this way, then that way. I knew all of the moves perfectly but I guess Girl needed to practice a bit more. I didn't mind helping her as long as she didn't keep me out in the sun too long. Finally she seemed satisfied that she remembered all the moves. We left the practicing and moved over to where several other pigs were also being walked and paused.

I didn't know any of them. They all looked shiny clean and brushed. Some of them even had ribbons around their necks.

"This is where you will be judged," said Girl and she placed me just so and stood stiffly beside me.

I looked around at the other pigs. Some of them looked like they would make good company but there really wasn't an opportunity to chat.

There was movement as people strolled here and there and chattered about this or that. I didn't pay much attention to it all. Soon I felt sleepy and just wished that I could stretch out in the warm sun and take a nap.

Girl didn't seem to want me to do that. Every now and then she leaned over and scratched my ear or stroked my back or just spoke to me.

Soon a little group moved over to us and Girl asked me to stand and walk, then pause, then turn this way and that way. I helped her through this practice too. We walked back to our spot. The small group of chattering people moved along with us, sizing me up from every angle. I was even touched by a hand several times. Then the little group moved on.

Girl let me lie down then. I guess she didn't need any more practice. And she could see that I was tired.

It seemed a long time later when the little group came back our way again. One of them stepped forward, said some words and handed Girl a bit of blue ribbon. I couldn't see anything special about it, but Girl sure got excited.

"We did it. We did it," she cried to the grinning Man and Woman. The two boys jumped up and down and clapped their hands, shouting right along with Girl. They all seemed awfully excited about something.

I was taken back to my pen and given some of the special food. Only Girl stayed with me.

"You did it, Porky," she said to me. She still had the annoying habit of calling me Porky. "You won the Blue Ribbon. I am so proud of you." And she hugged me around the neck. "Do you know what that means? It means that you were the very best pig in the show - Junior Section."

The very best pig in the show - Junior Section. I didn't understand exactly what that meant, but I knew that it was something to be proud of. I could feel my chest swell. I could hardly wait to get home and tell my family members, especially Hawkins. I knew that he would be green with envy. And I also knew that all of the others would

be so proud of me.

We rode home again at the end of the day. I was glad to see the new, red barn. I was even gladder to see my own special pen. I couldn't wait to tell my family about my special day - to tell them about the ribbon and how happy Girl had been that I was the best in the show.

As soon as I was back in my pen, I crowded up to the boards. They were all waiting for me on the other side.

"Where have you been?" Higgins demanded. "We thought you weren't coming back."

"I was at the Fair," I informed them all with a bit of a swagger. "Remember, Girl chose me."

"Fair? What was it like?"

"People. And animals. And noise. Lots of noise. Everyone was moving about and dogs were barking, cats meowing, sheep bleating, geese honking - all at the same time."

"It must have been awful," said Othelia.

I grinned. "No. It was exciting. Really exciting. I quite enjoyed it."

"What did you do there?" asked Millie, or Tillie.

"I...I..." I could hardly wait to share my great news. I puffed out my chest and lifted my chin higher. "I won a Blue Ribbon," I blurted out excitedly, sure that they would all cheer my accomplishment.

"A Blue Ribbon? For what?" asked Hawkins.

"For being the best pig at the fair - Junior Section," I hastened to say. Now I was really swaggering with the importance of my deed. I watched for their reaction, sure that they must be awed by my achievement.

My news was followed by silence. No one was cheering. Six pairs of eyes stared blankly at me.

"So where is this Blue Ribbon?" asked Hawkins and my chest returned quickly to normal size.

"Girl has it," I answered rather defensively.

"I thought you said you won it," said Hawkins.

"I did! That is...I did! Honest."

"Then why does Girl have it?"

"I won it. Honest. It means that I was the best pig at the Fair - Junior Section. Girl said so."

"What do you do with a Blue Ribbon?" asked Bee-Bee. At least she sounded a little interested.

"I...I don't...don't really know," I stumbled. Girl has it."

Othelia began to laugh. "Can you eat a Blue Ribbon?" she asked me in a teasing voice.

"No," I answered crossly. I was angry that they were spending all their time concentrating on the Blue Ribbon rather than on my achievement.

"Is it big enough and soft enough to sleep on?" chimed in Tillie, or Millie.

I didn't even answer that.

"What do you do with it?" asked Othelia.

"I...I don't know. But Girl has it. She was really happy about it. The whole family danced and clapped and..."

"Hiram," said Othelia with deliberation. "You are just a pig like the rest of us. Just the same. No different."

"Yeah," joined in Hawkins, "you are a pig like the rest of us. Best pig at the Fair. Phooey! Notice, they didn't take me."

"Or me!"

"Or me!"

I had felt proud and puffed up but I sure wasn't anymore. I pulled my snout back from the boards of the pen and retreated to the far corner. I flopped down in the straw still hearing the jeering and teasing that was coming from next door.

"Hiram thinks he's special. Hiram thinks he's special. He's just a pig. Only a pig like the rest of us."

I buried my head in the straw and tried to go to sleep. I had never felt so lonely in my whole life.

In the next few days I did an awful lot of serious thinking. Finally I came to the conclusion that my family and their opinion of me was far more important to me than I had realized. I had spent all of my growing-up time vying for first place. Hawkins had always been bigger so I felt that I had to be better. I figured that if I finally managed to outdo him, it would make me feel pretty good.

Now I had won best pig in the show - Junior Section, and I didn't feel good at all. In fact, I felt downright terrible. Terrible and lonesome. My own family ignored me, except to throw another taunt my way now and then.

Eventually I began to see that much of my trouble was my own fault. I had come home from the Fair feeling pretty big for my breeches. I had bragged and strutted and acted like a real jerk. No wonder they were all fed up with me. They were right, of course. I was a pig. Just an ordinary pig like the rest of them. I was no better and no worse. I had just been given special favors and special care. That was what had enabled me to win at the Fair. That, plus all of the help and instructions that Girl had given me. I began to feel ashamed of myself for acting so high and mighty.

They still teased me.

"Well, how is Mr. Blue Ribbon today?" they would say.

"I see Mr. Blue Ribbon is still living in a pig pen."

"Where's your piece of Blue? Haven't you got it from Girl yet?"

I hated the teasing but I realized that I had it coming. At last I walked straight over to the boards and poked my snout through to talk to them.

"You are right," I admitted. "I am just a pig, an ordinary pig. I...I was just...just treated special and...and fed special and trained to...to do the things that Girl wanted me to do. I have nothing to be proud of. Nothing."

There was silence.

"I'm...I'm sorry for acting so...so cocky about the Blue Ribbon," I continued. "Please...please can we...can we forget all about it?"

It was Bee-Bee who spoke up first. "I think it's nice that you won the ribbon," she said frankly. "It should make us all feel a little proud."

Tillie and Millie both lowered their eyes and then looked up to nod slowly.

"You...you worked hard," admitted Othelia, "you and Girl. I...I guess you deserved - something."

Higgins came right up to me and touched his snout against mine.

"I would have given it to you," he grunted. "I think you look great."

Only Hawkins made no move toward me.

"Then can we forget about it?" I prompted. "And be friends again?"

They all nodded and I went back to my feeding trough feeling much, much better.

But I still did a lot of thinking.

"Yes, I am still a pig. I am no better than the rest of them. But I have been given special treatment, special care and special training. That...that should make me, well, it should make me different than I would have been without it."

At last I got it worked out in my thinking. I was a pig. I was not better than other pigs but, because of all the special things that had happened in my life, I should be the best pig that I could possibly be. I sort of owed it to Girl. I even owed it to my mother, my family, and myself. I felt much better when I finally sorted it through and accepted the new Hiram.

There was still one thing that bothered me. Hawkins.

Hawkins hadn't accepted my apology. Hawkins had always hoped that he would be the one chosen for the Fair. Perhaps he should have been. He had always been bigger than me. And he had been a good brother. Sure, we always tried to outdo one another. But we had shared some fun times, too. I wished with all of my heart that there was some way for me to make peace with Hawkins.

One day I was surprised from my nap by someone entering my pen. Man was there and he gently eased something over the boards and lowered it to the floor of the pen. I looked up, blinking. There was Hawkins.

"There," said Man, "you can stay here for a few days until you feel better." He straightened up and was gone.

I arose from my bed and moved toward Hawkins. He stood shaking, his head hanging down.

"What happened?" I asked.

Hawkins took a few steps toward me. He was limping. I could tell that he didn't want to talk about it.

"I got caught in the fence," was all he said.

I nodded and didn't ask any more questions.

"Want a drink?" I asked him. "There is water there in the trough."

Hawkins moved slowly toward the trough and lowered his head for a long drink of cool water.

I couldn't help but feel surprise as I looked at him. I was bigger than he was. I thought of all the times that he had pushed me around, always wanting to be first, always wanting the most and the best. I looked back at my brother. He needed me. Needed the warmth of my straw bed and the coolness of my watering trough.

"Girl should soon be here with our dinner," I

said softly.

Hawkins nodded.

"You can eat first," I went on. "I'm not too hungry."

Hawkins looked at me, then at the trough. "There is room for both of us," he said and I nodded.

"Do you want a nap?" I asked him.

"That would be good," answered Hawkins. He hobbled over to the straw bed in the corner.

I waited until he was comfortably settled before I curled up beside him.

"Tell me if I hurt your sore leg," I said.

Hawkins just grunted and stretched out his head to rest it on my shoulder. Together the two of us snuggled in the straw.

I was almost asleep when Hawkins spoke. His voice was so low that I could hardly hear him, yet the words came to me with a quiet firmness.

"Hiram?"

I grunted in answer.

"You...you really deserved that Blue Ribbon."

I grinned to myself and moved a little closer to my brother, my friend.

Artist   Dedication

In appreciation, illustrations dedicated to
Stephen Frantz, Beth Ann Bauters and
Jared Bauters for posing with pigs;
and to Jill and Roland Rohrer
for sharing their pigs.